Praise for
To Catch a Thief

"*To Catch a Thief* is a page-turner of a mystery with a great big heart, and Amelia MacGuffin is the smart, funny kid sleuth we've all been waiting for. Readers will laugh and fall in love with the MacGuffin family as they follow the clues to crack this absolutely delightful case."
—Kate Messner, *New York Times* bestselling author of *Breakout*

"Get ready to have your heart stolen. With its wit and warmth, this treasure of a book deserves to be on every bookshelf next to the Penderwicks and *Because of Winn-Dixie*." —Justina Chen, author of *Lovely, Dark, and Deep*

"*To Catch a Thief* isn't just a fascinating and ever-deepening mystery. It's also a testament to the power of telling the right story the right way, and the transformative love of an absurdly charming dog." —Eliot Schrefer, *New York Times* bestselling author of the Lost Rainforest series

"This is the kind book I loved as a kid—and still love now. The kind you read once through to figure out the mystery and then over and over again so you can spend more time with Amelia and the rest of the MacGuffins, drinking proper hot chocolate, cuddling Doc, and solving thrilling crimes." —Linda Urban, author of *A Crooked Kind of Perfect*

"*To Catch a Thief* is the coziest of mysteries, a love letter to families and neighbors, the story of a very good dog, and further proof that Martha Brockenbrough can write whatever kind of book she wants to—and do it superbly." —Mike Jung, author of *The Boys in the Back Row*

"With a rare combination of wit and heart, Martha Brockenbrough crafts a charming mystery that celebrates the value of community, the power of finding your voice, and, best of all, the wonderful things that can happen when you have a very good dog at your side."
—Anne Ursu, author of *The Trouble Girls of Dragomir Academy*

TO CATCH A THIEF

Martha Brockenbrough

Scholastic Press / New York

Library of Congress Cataloging-in-Publication Data

Names: Brockenbrough, Martha, author.
Title: To catch a thief / Martha Brockenbrough.
Description: First edition. | New York : Scholastic Press, 2023. | Audience: Ages 8–12. | Audience: Grades 4–6. | Summary: Eleven-year-old Amelia thinks of herself as devoid of talent, but when the dragonfly staff goes missing seven days before the Dragonfly Day Festival, she takes it upon herself to catch the thief and save her town.
Identifiers: LCCN 2022021341 (print) | LCCN 2022021342 (ebook) | ISBN 9781338818581 (hardcover) | ISBN 9781338818598 (ebook)
Subjects: LCSH: Theft—Juvenile fiction. | Festivals—Juvenile fiction. | Dogs—Juvenile fiction. | Brothers and sisters—Juvenile fiction. | Self-confidence—Juvenile fiction. | Detective and mystery stories. | CYAC: Mystery and detective stories. | Stealing—Fiction. | Festivals—Fiction. | Dogs—Fiction. | Brothers and sisters—Fiction. | Self-confidence—Fiction. | BISAC: JUVENILE FICTION / Family / General (see also headings under Social Themes) | JUVENILE FICTION / Mysteries & Detective Stories | LCGFT: Detective and mystery fiction.
Classification: LCC PZ7.B7825 To 2023 (print) | LCC PZ7.B7825 (ebook) | DDC 813.6 [Fic]—dc23/eng/20220613

10 9 8 7 6 5 4 3 2 1   23 24 25 26 27

Printed in Italy   183

First edition, April 2023

Book design by Stephanie Yang

To Elana K. Arnold,
a partner in crime

1

So It Begins . . .

A thief stood at the edge of a charming but run-down village. Cars sped by. The thief took a deep breath. From one direction came the scents of salt water, washed-up kelp, and dead crabs. From the other, fresh bread, crackling fires, herb gardens, and even a few rosebushes.

The town smelled good. As if it could be home.

The air smelled of something else too. Rain.

All the better, the thief observed. Rain drives people indoors. Rain is almost as good as the cover of darkness when it comes to thieving.

The first drops spiraled downward. Then more. Soon it became a downpour, drumming the gravel on the shoulder of the highway, gathering in murky puddles.

The thief, now drenched, left the road and passed a sign that read WELCOME TO URCHIN BEACH.

1

Below that, a second sign read COUNTDOWN TO THE WORLD-FAMOUS DRAGONFLY DAY FESTIVAL.

And below that, a third sign showed the number 7. A lucky number, as just about anyone will tell you.

The thief paid no attention to the signs.

That's because the thief had spied something wonderful.

Something they wanted.

Something they would take.

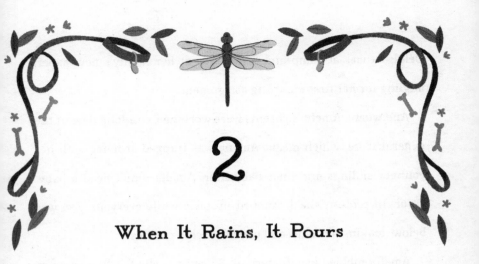

2

When It Rains, It Pours

Amelia MacGuffin thought of rainy days as mystery weather. She liked the way a good rain blurred the edges of things. How it seemed to tap secret codes against the roof. Rain also felt *cozy*, which happens to be a type of mystery that takes place in a small community and is solved by an amateur detective. Amelia wished this sort of thing would happen in her town—to her, even. Not that it ever would.

One drizzly Saturday in August, she was reading in the window seat of the turret in her crooked, old house. She set down her book. She already knew how it ended. Usually knowing the ending comforted her. But now it made her feel stuck.

Sixth grade was starting in two weeks. She should have been with her two best friends, mapping out their survival strategy. But

Delphine was at camp and Birdie was at her family's newspaper, angling for her first reporting assignment.

And worse, Amelia's parents were working extra-long days at the general store, which meant Amelia was trapped at home with her younger siblings and their babysitter. Amelia didn't need a babysitter. In protest, she'd tromped upstairs while everyone else was below, making a ruckus and chocolate chip cookies.

Amelia nibbled at a fingernail. Sometimes she felt like an extra character in a book, the unimportant sort described as "the boy with the blue shirt" or "the girl with the rainbow braces."

All around her were more interesting people living more daring lives. Delphine had moved here from Taiwan when she was three and had just headed to a summer camp for young oceanographers. Birdie was an indirect descendant of Martin Luther King Jr. and took pictures for the *Urchin Beach Gazette*. She planned to become a real live reporter there before she turned twelve. Amelia's sister Bridget was an acrobat, her brother Colin was an inventor, and the twins, Duncan and Emma, were funny and adorable even if they couldn't use the toilet yet.

Amelia didn't have the gumption even for the littlest things. For example, she wanted to change the way her hair was parted.

Her current style felt babyish. But she was too nervous. What if people thought she was trying to be cooler than she was? What if people liked her old hair better?

Face it, she told herself. *You can't even win a battle with a comb.*

She rubbed smudges off her glasses and studied the winding streets below. Only a few people braved the rain. Even the crows and robins had taken shelter. On the other side of the room, a wide window framed a view of Dr. Agatha's manor. It was a grim and glowering edifice, separated from the MacGuffins' house by a thick hedge that shimmered with rainwater. A single light was on, the one in Dr. Agatha's study, where she wrote murder mysteries that were famous for their lengthy descriptions of death by unusual methods: rare poisons, buckets of concrete dropped from heights, evil deeds with construction equipment, and even suffocation by Marshmallow Fluff.

Write what you know. That's what Amelia's fourth-grade teacher, Mrs. Neuschwanger, had told them.

It made Amelia wonder how Dr. Agatha knew so much about murder. Amelia could only conclude that Dr. Agatha had killed before. Probably more than once. Thank goodness for the hedge between their houses. It wasn't a high stone wall, but it wasn't nothing.

Amelia turned back to her usual window as a moving truck rolled into view.

With a squeal of brakes, the truck stopped at the house across the street, which had been vacant for as long as she could remember. She gasped. New neighbors. She'd have to tell Birdie. Birdie would want to take photos for the newspaper. Delphine would also want to know, but her camp had a no-cell-phone rule and took place on a boat, so Amelia couldn't even send a letter. No matter. It would be a wonderful surprise for when she returned.

A family emerged. Two kids and a pair of women who looked motherish. The kids were twins, a boy and a girl—like Duncan and Emma. They had vibrant red hair that stood out in the gloom. But what made Amelia's skin prickle wasn't their hair. It was their age. They were seventh graders. She was sure of it. She, Birdie, and Delphine had a theory that seventh graders were the scariest people in middle school, but only because eighth graders no longer cared.

Before she could dial Birdie's number on the house landline, several sets of feet pounded the stairs. Bridget's footsteps, loud and certain. Colin's, careful and light. And then Duncan and Emma, taking the stairs one at a time because that's what toddlers do. They'd obviously seen the truck and were coming to her for a pronouncement on what it meant.

Amelia turned away from the window, folded her hands in her lap, and waited for the people she loved most in the world to arrive.

3

The Invisible Thief

The town square was empty when the thief arrived. The thief knew straightaway what to steal. The way the wooden staff rested in the arms of a giant wooden Sasquatch meant it was precious. It took the thief a moment to figure out how to remove it, but the thief had time.

No one was watching.

No one wanted to be out in the rain.

The few people hurrying past in their slickers and boots took no notice of the thief. The thief was used to invisibility. The thief counted on it. This was how the thief survived. This was what made the thief so good at stealing. The thief was good at other things too. But stealing, pinching, pilfering, absconding . . . these, the thief did without even thinking. They were as natural to the thief as grinning.

Later that day, when the crime was discovered by the mayor, it was a shock. A scandal. An outrage.

The only person slightly happy about it was Birdie Wheeler, who got to photograph the crime scene for a newspaper story. She couldn't wait to tell her friend Amelia all about it.

The thief, meanwhile, had vanished.

This didn't mean the thief had left town. Quite the opposite. The thief was settling in, drying off, and thinking about what to take next.

4

A Surprise in the Hedge

To most observers, the younger MacGuffin siblings looked as though they'd been shaken out of the same cereal box. They had the same sandy hair. The same light eyes and often suntanned white skin. Matching smiles and scabby knees from bike riding and tree climbing and fast runs down the oyster shell paths that wound through the village. All but Amelia, with her dark hair, pale face, and glasses. It was only Amelia's smile—friendly when it was genuine, tight when it was fake—that marked her as a MacGuffin too.

"We have new neighbors!" Bridget announced. Then she flipped over and crossed the room on her hands. Acrobatics and feats of strength were her special skills. Well, two of them. Bridget had many talents.

"I've already called the store," Colin said. "Mom and Dad are bringing home a bucket. I'm going to put in some nuts and bolts in case one of our new neighbors is also an inventor. Maybe some duct tape too."

The bucket was the standard housewarming gift from the MacGuffins. They filled it with assorted useful things: packets of seeds, dish towels, a hammer, and both kinds of screwdrivers.

"Bucket, bucket," the twins said. Then they laughed. Duncan and Emma loved words. They loved repeating them, and they loved laughing.

Amelia held out her hands. The twins climbed onto her lap, each of them holding half of a pale green blanket they'd shared their whole lives. Once they'd started walking, their father had cut the blanket in two to reduce tussles over it.

"Where's Maya?" Amelia asked. Maya was their babysitter.

"Writing another poem, duh," Bridget said. "I think this one is about the glory of rain." Maya often felt inspired to write poetry, especially about nature. The MacGuffin children had grown used to it. While Maya's poems were of mixed quality, Amelia and her siblings enjoyed the breaks from her enthusiastic supervision.

"I say we visit right away," Bridget said. "We can offer to help them unpack their boxes, and then we can see all their stuff."

Amelia wasn't so sure. "Why would you want to see all their stuff?"

"Why *wouldn't* I?" Bridget flipped back on her feet. "Stuff is my favorite thing."

"I'm not sure that's a good idea." Amelia worried that Bridget would make a spectacle of herself. "Not till Mom and Dad are home. And maybe not even then."

"I want to be the one to tell them about the Dragonfly Day Festival," Bridget said. "They'll thank me later."

"They probably already know," Amelia said. "Most people do."

It was true. Dragonfly Day was widely considered the best beach festival anywhere. There was delicious food, kite flying, a parade, and a contest to see who could spot the first green darner dragonfly. All the merchants in town contributed money to get people whipped into a frenzy. This year, the prize for spotting the first dragonfly was $1,000, the most it had ever been.

Green darners were not only the official state insect, they were also symbols of luck. To honor them, Urchin Beach had a special wooden staff with a brown spot on it that looked exactly like a dragonfly, right down to the leaded-glass-window pattern on its wings.

The staff was lucky. Every year, the mayor carried it when she was grand marshal of the Dragonfly Day parade. Thousands of tourists came from all over to replenish their own personal supplies of good fortune by paying five dollars each to swing the staff over their heads three times.

The people who did often enjoyed astonishing luck. Newspapers from as far away as Seattle, Los Angeles, New York City, and even Shanghai, Nairobi, and Paris had written about it. People who'd swung the staff at the festival had won the state lottery. A professional soccer player had led her team to a Major League Cup victory. A kitten that had gotten stuck in an eighty-foot poplar tree tumbled out and was caught by a kid who'd swung the staff. The kitten, who would have perished otherwise, was perfectly fine and was adopted by the very same kid who'd made the lucky catch.

Over the past century, the dragonfly staff had become a thing of legend. It was, without a doubt, the most important object in Urchin Beach. Some people argued that it should not be on display all year. That it was too risky. That it was hard on the wood. But the mayor thought otherwise.

"It's lasted a century and however long the tree lived before that," she said. "It deserves to be seen and enjoyed by everyone. You might even say that the spirit of the town is wrapped up in this stick. Hiding it away would diminish us all."

And, of course, the money it brought in every year during the

Dragonfly Day Festival made a big difference around town. It paid for sidewalks, parks, streets, and the library, and the tourists' enthusiastic shopping during the festival helped keep all the Urchin Beach businesses afloat the rest of the year.

On top of that, the festival was enormous fun. Amelia was counting the days, literally, until it arrived. Seven remained—an eternity.

"Anyway, I'll probably be the one to tell them about Dragonfly Day," she said. "Because I'm the oldest."

"Not if I get there first," Bridget said. "I'm the fastest."

The sisters might have launched an argument if Colin hadn't raised his hand and said, "There's something else. And it has nothing to do with Dragonfly Day."

"Don't hold out on us," Bridget said.

"Yes," Amelia said. "What is it?"

Colin clasped his hands over his heart and whispered, "There's a dog outside."

"I bet it's the new neighbors'," Bridget said. "We should offer to feed it when they go away on vacation. We should charge at least ten dollars a day, two for each of us, and—"

"I don't think it belongs to them," Colin interrupted.

Bridget did a back walkover. "How do you know?"

"Well." Colin was an observant sort. Still, he seemed hesitant.

"It's all right, Colin." Amelia meant it as much for him as she did for herself.

Colin lowered his voice even more. "The dog came out of the hedge at Dr. Agatha's house. There's a small hole at the base of it, not far from the shed. It's the sort of thing you wouldn't notice if you weren't looking for it."

A hole in the hedge—that was worrisome. The emergence of a dog from said hole was curious. Dr. Agatha did not have a dog. She'd never own one. Not in a million years. Dogs had even learned to stay out of her way on the sidewalk.

Amelia had a hunch. This dog was lost. It needed a new home. And, conveniently, the MacGuffins needed a dog. The older children sometimes put Mr. MacGuffin's socks on the twins' hands and feet and had them crawl around and bark, but it wasn't the same as a real dog. There was nothing they wanted more, but their parents had been firm: no dog. Not now, not ever. There was too much going on for them to manage one more living thing. Besides, the vet bills were too expensive.

Colin swallowed and licked his lips. "The dog crawled out before the moving truck arrived, and it's been hiding in the backyard since. Poor thing's covered in mud and shivering."

"That's terrible," Bridget said.

"Terrible," the twins said.

"Where do you think the dog came from?" Amelia asked.

It was a mystery. But it also felt like a gift. The dog she'd been waiting for had materialized in their yard, as if dragonfly luck had descended already. This was her opportunity to be the hero. To save the dog. To persuade her parents to adopt it. To raise money for its upkeep somehow.

She imagined herself strutting through town with the dog on a leash. She imagined it sleeping at the foot of her bed. She imagined teaching it tricks, like playing dead and walking on its hind legs while balancing a ball on its nose. Most of all, she imagined having an identity. She would be the girl with the exceptional canine.

"Let's go see this mysterious dog," Bridget said.

"What about Maya?" Colin asked.

"I have a plan," Amelia said.

"Plan," Duncan and Emma said.

"So," Amelia said. "Here's what we need to do."

Her siblings leaned in to listen.

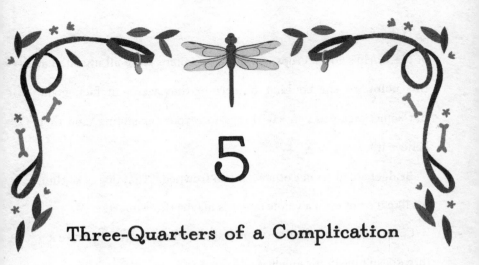

5

Three-Quarters of a Complication

The MacGuffin children stood in the backyard, looking at the saddest dog any of them had ever seen.

"Your plan's never gonna work," Bridget said, balancing on one leg.

Amelia took a deep breath. "It's worked so far," she said. "We got past Maya."

"That was easy. You gave her a plate of cookies and asked her to write us a golden shovel poem," Bridget said. "That'll take her at least an hour."

"I made it *look* easy," Amelia said. "Because I have a knack for plans and schemes." Her throat tightened—was she good at plans and schemes? She wasn't sure, although she often spent time inside her head planning what she would do if disaster struck. She even had disaster categories: alien invasion, zoo animal escape, failure of the world's cocoa crops, tsunami. Her plans were all untested at this point, so she couldn't be certain they were, in fact, good. But sometimes you can say things to a younger sibling, and they believe it.

Bridget stood on her other leg and frowned. "That dog is so thin, it's like it's not even a whole dog. It's maybe three-quarters."

Colin raised one of his extremely skinny fingers. "Just because it's thin doesn't mean it's any less of a dog."

"Three-quarters of a dog," Amelia repeated slowly. "Bridget—that's it!"

"That's it," Duncan and Emma said. "That's it!"

"I don't get it," Bridget said.

"I think what Amelia means," Colin said, "is that Mom and Dad haven't expressly forbidden us to adopt *three-quarters* of a dog. We could even argue that adopting an unfortunate creature is the humane thing to do, regardless of its size. You know how insistent our parents are on doing the right thing."

"Well, the dog is disgusting," Bridget said. "It's all covered in mud. If that even is mud. It smells totally suspect."

"We could give it a bath to create the best possible first impression," Colin said. "First impressions are important."

Amelia paced. "Let me think."

18

Colin had made an excellent point. But a bath seemed impossible. To wash the dog, they'd first have to bring it inside. And to do *that*, they'd have to get it past Maya, which wouldn't be easy. Even mid-golden shovel, she'd probably put down her fountain pen if she saw a live animal.

But first, they were going to need to catch the dog. It looked fast.

"We need a collar and a leash," Amelia said.

"Where are we supposed to get those?" Bridget asked.

"The general store," Colin said.

"We can't go there," Bridget said. "Mom and Dad would want to know why we wanted a collar and a leash."

Amelia nodded. "We'll have to lure it."

"Lure it?" Colin asked.

"With food," Amelia said. "It's probably hungry."

"Dogs can always eat," Bridget said. "It is a fact. We should use a cheese stick." She stood on her hands, using the welcome mat for padding.

Amelia knew better than to question a Bridget fact. "Let's check the fridge."

"Fridge," Duncan said.

Emma laughed. "Fridge."

In the kitchen, Amelia considered the problem of Maya. Even if Maya was immersed in her poem, she would most likely notice a wet and muddy dog. The situation called for improvisation.

"Duncan and Emma," Amelia said. "Can you wet your diapers?"

"Yes," Emma said.

"Already did," Duncan said.

"Excellent. Colin and Bridget, go get some cheese. We'll meet back here."

In the family room, Amelia handed the wet twins off to Maya. Then she returned to Colin and Bridget in the kitchen. Their hands were full of peeled cheese sticks.

"You can't give the dog all the cheese," Amelia said. "That's for snacks."

"It'll take the cheese it takes," Bridget said.

She had a point.

"Should we wear raincoats?" Colin asked.

"There's no time," Amelia said. "We have only as long as the span of two diaper changes."

They stepped outside. The MacGuffins' backyard was large, with a vegetable garden on one side and a swing set on the other. A path cut through the middle, lined with clumps of herbs: rosemary, sage, oregano, and thyme. Puddles prickled with raindrops, and the air was so thick with moisture it looked gray.

Colin scanned the yard. "Where did he go?"

"How do we know it's a boy?" Bridget asked. "It's sexist to assume."

"There's a way to tell," Colin said.

"Gross," Bridget said. "Never mind."

"He went back into the hedge," Colin said. "Right through that hole."

"Here, dog!" Bridget waved the cheese.

"Shh," Amelia said.

"Who's going to hear?" Bridget said.

"Everybody," Amelia said. But what she meant was Dr. Agatha.

"Here he comes," Colin said. "Look."

"The moment of cheese," Bridget said. "Let's roll."

Amelia gestured to her siblings to hold still. Bridget shrugged and complied.

A black nose wiggled. Bright brown eyes gleamed. The dog crawled all the way out. He was drenched, muddy, and made of bones. It was hard to tell what color he was, but his fur was longish and matted. Bridget crouched and offered a cheese stick. He sniffed it and then took it gently in his mouth. He wagged his tail and looked at Bridget, as if to ask for more. She gave him another.

"Don't just give him cheese," Amelia said. "Lure him."

"So bossy," Bridget said. But she stood anyway.

The three of them inched backward toward the house, giving the dog tiny bits of cheese as they went. Once they made it inside, Amelia realized she should have fetched a towel. Or several. The dog was dripping muddy water all over the floor and leaving paw prints everywhere he stepped. There was only one thing to do. She picked him up. Her T-shirt was immediately soaked. The dog was heavier than he looked. This was going to be a tough climb to the third floor, where the bathtub was.

She grunted. "Cover me."

Bridget and Colin exchanged a glance that said, *There is only one way to do this.*

They headed for the stairs.

"Maya," Colin called, with what Amelia knew was his fake voice, "will you please read us your golden shovel poem as slowly as possible so we can savor every word?"

Maya's voice traveled. "I'd love to," she said. "But first, can you help me get these diapers back on the twins? They keep saying it's naked time, and it's definitely not."

Amelia reached the bathroom, and soon the glug and chug of

water running into the claw-foot tub covered the sound of Maya's poetry reading. Amelia helped the dog in and started soaping his fur. She could tell that he didn't like it, but she could also tell that he was a very good boy. He was medium size, with triangular ears that stood all the way up, except for their tips. His paws were huge, and she wondered whether he still had puppy in him.

She rinsed out the soap and discovered reddish patches of fur on his chest and shoulders. The color reminded her of the twins who'd moved in next door. She realized she still hadn't told Birdie about them. Amelia let out a huge breath. There was so much to do, all of it nerve-racking. Was this how her parents felt every day? If so, then growing up was one more thing to keep her awake at night.

After the dog was as clean as she could get him, she pulled the plug. The brown, sudsy water swirled down the drain, and the dog shook himself violently. Bathwater flew everywhere, spattering her glasses and soaking her shirt. She thought he was having an attack of some sort. Then she realized he was drying himself off.

"We use towels in this house," Amelia said. She wrapped him in a clean one and started rubbing him dry, scrunching her forehead as she did. She'd thought she'd feel better once he was clean. Like she'd be able to see the light at the end of the tunnel. But that wasn't the case. Instead, it felt as though the tunnel were squeezing her and making it hard to breathe. She resolved to chew a fingernail as soon as she'd washed her hands.

None of the rest of the MacGuffins seemed bothered by the weight of the world this way. To them, skinny dogs and new neighbors weren't a worry—they felt like possibility. Amelia sometimes wished she could swap lives with someone who worried less and enjoyed life more.

As she finished toweling the dog, Colin and Bridget joined her, each leading a twin.

"I kind of liked the golden shovel," Colin said. "If an inventor were to write a poem, that would probably be the sort. The way the last words in the line are made of another poem is so innovative."

"Not me," Bridget said. "Golden shovels can shove off. We told Maya that we all wanted sandwiches, preferably triple-decker. That ought to keep her busy."

"He looks really different clean," Colin said.

"Still a toothpick," Bridget said.

Amelia hugged the dog. He was trembling, from cold or fear, she couldn't tell. But she felt every one of his ribs, and this made her love him more.

"Doc!" Duncan said.

"Doc!" Emma said.

They both laughed.

Bridget scratched the dog's chin. "Who's a good dog? Who's a good dog? You are."

The dog looked surprised to hear it. It made Amelia worry about him. About what he might have suffered that he doubted his goodness.

"He's even cuter than I realized," Colin said. "I thought he was all brown, but look! He has a white spot on his chest, and it's shaped like a heart."

"We need to come up with a name for him," Bridget said. "I vote Muffin."

The dog did not look like a Muffin.

"What about Bert?" Colin said.

That was closer.

"Doc!" Duncan said.

"Doc!" Emma said.

"Yes," Amelia said. "He is a dog."

"I don't think that's what they're saying," Bridget said. "I think they're saying 'Doc.'"

Doc. The dog cocked his head and thumped his tail.

"I think he likes that name," Colin said.

"Mom has always wanted a doctor in the family," Bridget said. "This will help our case."

Amelia had her doubts. But they were in too deep now.

Bridget cocked her head and looked at him. "We should brush him. He looks disheveled."

"I'll clean the bathroom," Amelia said. "You guys untangle his fur. Use Dad's brush. He won't notice."

Then she planted a kiss on the dog's head, and he kissed her cheek in return.

"Good boy, Doc," Amelia said. "Good boy." She knew right then if they weren't allowed to keep him, she would never forgive herself.

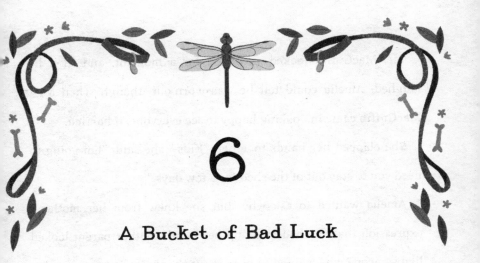

6

A Bucket of Bad Luck

The rain did not relent. It fell as the children took turns keeping Doc quiet in the turret. It fell as Maya made them cocoa with graham crackers. It fell as Mr. MacGuffin returned home from work carrying a wet WELCOME TO URCHIN BEACH bucket.

He set it beside the door as he slipped off his dripping galoshes. Then he paid Maya, who peeled Duncan and Emma off her legs and waved goodbye.

"Where's Mom?" Colin asked.

"She said she had to stash something," Mr. MacGuffin said. "She won't be long."

"What did she have to stash?" Amelia asked.

"She didn't say," Mr. MacGuffin said. "She is a woman of secrets and mystery."

"Are you sure you're talking about our mother?" Bridget asked.

Mr. MacGuffin looked surprised for a moment, and then he laughed. Amelia could tell he was worn-out, though. Then Mrs. MacGuffin came in, looking happy to see everyone, if harried.

She clapped her hands together. "Kids," she said, "I'm going to need you to stay out of the shed for a few days."

Amelia wanted to ask why. But she knew from her mother's expression that she had made up her mind. Neither parent looked like someone who wanted to hear about the three-quarters of a dog their five children had found in the backyard. They looked like people who needed to sit by the fire with their feet up. Amelia whispered into Colin's ear, and he ran to the kitchen to plug in the teakettle.

"Why don't you sit?" Amelia said to her parents.

"Yes," Bridget said. "Take a load off, and then we can show you our surprise."

"Surprise?" Mr. MacGuffin said.

"What surprise?" Mrs. MacGuffin asked.

"Doc," Emma said.

"Doc," Duncan said.

Amelia cringed. "Sit down, sit down! Colin is making some tea. Won't that be ni—"

"We rescued a dog!" Bridget interrupted. "And we gave him a bath and groomed him with Dad's brush."

"Bridget!" Amelia hissed.

"Oh, right. We rescued *most* of a dog."

The MacGuffin parents sank onto the couch.

"Most of a dog?" Mrs. MacGuffin asked.

"Three-quarters," Bridget said.

"My brush?" Mr. MacGuffin asked. Then he shrugged.

Colin entered with two steaming mugs. "Who wants tea?"

"I'd love some," Bridget said.

"It's for Mom and Dad," Amelia said.

Bridget harrumphed. "He asked who wanted it, though."

"Bridget," Mr. MacGuffin said. "Where is this partial dog?"

Colin stopped walking, sloshing tea on the floor. "She told them?"

"Amelia?" Mrs. MacGuffin said.

Amelia knew what her mother meant. *You are the oldest. You are responsible for whatever has happened. Never mind that we paid someone else to watch your brothers and sisters. The job is yours and always will be.*

She took a deep breath. "Colin found him in Dr. Agatha's hedge. He was wet—"

"The dog, not me," Colin interrupted.

"The dog was wet," Amelia continued. "And he was dirty and cold, and when we saw that he was extremely hungry, we knew we had to do something."

"He probably belongs to someone," Mr. MacGuffin said.

"Most likely Dr. Agatha," Mrs. MacGuffin said.

"He doesn't have a collar," Bridget said. "And Dr. Agatha dislikes dogs."

Dr. Agatha disliked everything. Amelia once passed her on the sidewalk, and Dr. Agatha pretended as though she hadn't seen her. But Amelia knew she had because she muttered, "MacGuffins are insignificant. That's the problem. That's the trouble with trying to use one." It was the rudest thing she'd ever heard.

"We thought it unlikely that anyone would want such a skinny dog," Amelia said. Her fingernails itched in a way that made her want to bite them.

"Anybody but us," Colin said. "We love him."

"We've named him," Bridget said.

"What did you name him?" Mr. MacGuffin asked.

"Dave!" Mrs. MacGuffin said. "They'll get attached."

"Doc," Duncan said.

"Doc," Emma said.

"Doc," Amelia, Bridget, and Colin said.

"Doc?" Mr. and Mrs. MacGuffin said.

There was a bark. And then Doc galloped in, his ears high, his tail wagging. He walked straight to Mrs. MacGuffin and put his front paws on her lap. Then he licked her face and she laughed.

"So this is Doc," Mr. MacGuffin said.

"Can we keep him?" Colin asked.

"Oh, I don't know," Mr. MacGuffin said.

"Is he even trained?" Mrs. MacGuffin asked.

Doc sat. He lifted a paw. He cocked his head to the side. By Amelia's reckoning, that was three separate skills. He was not only trained, he was a prodigy. She'd have him walking on his hind legs in no time.

There was silence in the room. Outside, raindrops sounded like the drumming fingers of someone thinking hard, someone unable to make up their mind. Amelia wanted to ask her parents when they would decide. What process they would use. Whether there was anything she could do to help sway them. But she knew not to ask.

Their mother spoke first. "Kids, it's been a long day. You've put us on the spot here with this dog."

"His name is Doc," Bridget said.

"We're sorry," Colin said. "We didn't know what else to do. He was in trouble."

"You did the right thing," Mr. MacGuffin said. "And now we have to decide where to go from here. We first have to look for his owner. If he doesn't have one, we can see if anyone else wants to take him in."

That wasn't a no, Amelia thought. If he had no owner and if no one else wanted him, how could her parents refuse?

The sky outside the windows flashed white. A few seconds later, a boom followed.

"Bridget, Amelia," Mr. MacGuffin said.

Amelia braced herself. That tone meant chores were coming.

"Girls," Mr. MacGuffin said. "Someone needs to take the house-warming bucket to the new neighbors. Will you please do that?"

"Yes!" Bridget said.

"Yes," Amelia said.

The same word but with entirely different meanings behind it. Bridget had been eager to see inside the house. To examine the neighbors' stuff and tell them about Dragonfly Day. Amelia was stating a simple fact. Yes, she would do what her father asked. But she did not want to.

The sky flashed white again. Another boom. Amelia and Bridget put on their raincoats and galoshes, hoisted the bucket, and went out into the storm.

7

It Was Not a Distress Signal

Rain drummed the sidewalk. It hissed and glittered in the weak light from the streetlamps. *Turn back*, it seemed to whisper. *Turn back*. Amelia wanted to, but she couldn't. If they were going to keep Doc, she had to do everything her parents asked, without any complaints.

Bridget held the bucket. "Ready?"

"Yes." This time, the word meant, *As ready as I'll ever be*.

The sisters looked both ways. They crossed the street.

The first-floor windows of their new neighbors' home were dark. Foreboding, even. A rusting porch light dangled from its wires.

"Maybe we should turn back," Amelia said.

"They're home. The upstairs lights are on," Bridget said.

"We could leave the bucket."

"Are you kidding? It might get washed away."

"It's a rainstorm, Bridget, not a tidal wave. Besides, it's a covered porch."

"We're supposed to tell them about the coupon for ten percent off at the Pacific General Store inside," Bridget said.

That last part was true. But Amelia didn't see why she couldn't tell them about this later. "They might not want to be disturbed."

"A bucket is not a disturbance. Buckets make everything better. This bucket will be the best thing that happens to them all day."

"There isn't a doorbell," Amelia said.

"That's why we're going to knock. Why *you're* going to knock. I have my hands full of bucket."

Amelia rapped quickly. *Tap, tap, tap.*

"Louder. They'll never hear that," Bridget said. "Do it like this." She set down the bucket and gave three long, loud, slow knocks. And then she imitated Amelia's three soft, quick ones. "You knocked like a baby bunny."

"Bunnies would never knock on a door," Amelia said. "They're prey animals. Very shy. And their knuckles are furry—"

The windows lit up. The door flew open.

"Who's in distress?" The redheaded twins stood there. One was a boy, and one was a girl. Both had light brown skin.

"Here's a bucket." Bridget held it up proudly.

"Welcome to Urchin Beach," Amelia said. "Our family owns the Pacific General Store, which has everything every kind of family needs, and this is a housewarming gift for you. Well, more for your moms. But there is a coupon inside, and it's good for ten percent off everything, including candy, comics, puzzles, and games."

"But who's in distress?" the girl asked again.

"Not me," Bridget said. "Watch." She did a back walkover. "Could someone in distress do *that?*"

Amelia said nothing. She *was* in distress. But how did this kid know? Was picking up secret distress signals her superpower?

"One of you knocked an SOS," the boy said. "Were you crying wolf?"

"There are no wolves in Urchin Beach," Bridget said. "But there are dragonflies, raccoons, and the occasional black bear—"

"SOS is a signal used by ships in extreme distress at sea," the girl interrupted. "It's Morse code."

"I knocked," Amelia said. "But I'm not in extreme distress." This was medium distress, not that it was anyone's business. "Any cry for help was inadvertent. We're here to give you a bucket."

Bridget set it at the feet of the twins.

The girl lifted the bucket. "Oh wow! I do love a bucket. Wanna come in?"

"Do I ever," Bridget said at the same time that Amelia said, "We should probably go home."

The twins laughed. This was the way Duncan and Emma were going to be in about ten years, Amelia thought. She liked the sound of their laughs. Even so, she really, really didn't want to go in.

"Don't be impolite, Amelia," Bridget said. "We'd love to shake the rain off a bit. Maybe put our feet up. Get to know what's in your boxes—I mean, each other."

The twins stepped aside, and Bridget and Amelia entered.

"Whoa! It's as creepy on the inside as it is on the outside," Bridget said.

Amelia gasped. "Bridget!"

"There's nothing wrong with creepy," Bridget said. "I plan to make that my high school aesthetic. I'm going to be the world's creepiest acrobat." She demonstrated with a handstand split while she crossed her eyes. Amelia had to give her credit. It was unsettling.

"She's not wrong about this place being creepy," the girl said. "This house is as creepy as a spider with wax lips. But our moms call it charming. They say the place has good bones."

"It would be gross if they were actual bones," the boy said. "We wouldn't be surprised if we found some in the walls, though. I'm kind of looking forward to that. It will be a mystery to solve."

His sister nodded.

Amelia liked this brother and sister. She liked that they seemed to be fans of mysteries. She wanted them to like her too, which made her feel scared all over again. Seventh graders *never* liked sixth graders. It was an unwritten rule. And the sister had her hair parted the way Amelia wanted hers to be, so she'd probably think Amelia was too babyish to befriend.

"I'm Dorothy," the girl said. "My brother is Dashiell. You can call us Dot and Dash. We're half of the Morse family."

Dorothy and Dashiell were the most romantic names Amelia had ever heard. She wished she could call them that instead of Dot and Dash.

"I'm Bridget, and my sister's Amelia. We also have twins at home. Duncan and Emma." Then Bridget walked over to an old-time radio. It was the size of a dishwasher, made of wood and shiny tortoiseshell plastic, with dials that read AM and FM. "Does this thing work?"

"Dunno," Dash said. "It was left behind. We haven't even plugged it in yet. The cord was frayed, so we have to fix it first."

Amelia immediately thought about how much Colin would love to repair the cord. She wondered what else had been left behind. The scuffed walls had hooks on them, as though they'd once held pictures. It was too dark to see into the corners—there was a single overhead light. But it looked as though there were some dusty lamps and chairs, along with a set of elaborate fireplace pokers. In a cozy mystery, those would undoubtedly be murder weapons.

Cardboard boxes lined the edges of the room. Bridget appeared to be trying to burn a hole through them with her eyes. Any minute and she was going to ask what was inside.

"Well," Amelia said, "we should be getting home."

"Are you sixth graders?" Bridget asked. "You look like sixth graders."

"Seventh," Dot said. "Middle of the middle school sandwich."

Bridget laughed like it was the funniest thing anyone had ever said. And it was funny. But Amelia would never have laughed out loud, lest they think she was laughing *at* them.

"What about you two?" Dash asked. "Sixth grade?"

"She's almost sixth, I'm almost fifth," Bridget said. "But I'm advanced. I'm also strong and flexible."

"I can tell," Dot said.

Amelia wondered whether Dot was teasing. She supposed it didn't matter if Bridget's feelings hadn't been hurt. Then there were footsteps on the stairs, and two women wearing sweatpants and bandannas appeared.

"Well, hello," the one with glasses said. "Who have we here?"

"Bridget and Amelia," Dot said. "And these are our moms, Kelly and Jiera." Kelly and Jiera looked nice. Kelly had glasses, strawberry-blonde hair in braids, and the kind of skin that looked like it needed a lot of sunscreen. Jiera had darker skin and long, thick, black hair. Amelia thought she might be of Indian heritage.

"They brought us a bucket," Dash said.

"A bucket," Kelly said. "There's nothing better than a bucket. Except maybe a stick. I do love a good stick. You can use it as a lever. To poke a campfire. To create an impromptu tent in a storm."

"Mama." Dot's cheeks were red. "Enough with the stick talk. It's embarrassing."

"She's embarrassing herself, not us," Dash said. Then he put his arm around Kelly's waist, and she gave him a noogie. Amelia was going to have so much to tell Birdie.

"Thank you for the bucket," Kelly said.

"Yes, it is delightful. And all these handy things inside," Jiera said.

Amelia nudged Bridget in the ribs. Then Bridget reminded them about the coupon.

On their way home, Bridget said, "I didn't mention the Dragonfly Day Festival. That way, I'll have an excuse to go back tomorrow and look in more boxes."

The house phone was ringing when Bridget and Amelia walked in the front door.

Colin answered. "Amelia," he said, "it's for you. Birdie."

When Amelia got on the line, Birdie didn't even say hi. She asked, "Did you know that only forty percent of American families still have phones like yours?"

Birdie knew many facts, probably even more than Bridget did. It was a side effect of spending so much time at the *Urchin Beach Gazette*, which subscribed to a newswire, a service that piped in stories from all around the world, everything from sports to science to advice.

"I didn't know that," Amelia said. "Did that come in on the business wire?"

"Tech wire," Birdie said. "I wish we had better cell service here. You sound like you're chewing popcorn."

"I wish I had popcorn," Amelia said. "And a cell phone." Then she sighed. "My parents won't get me one, though. Too expensive."

With five kids, the MacGuffins were always on a budget. The Pacific General Store that her parents ran was popular, but Mr. and Mrs. MacGuffin couldn't bear to make much of a profit, not when it was their neighbors buying necessities there.

"But that's not why I'm calling," Birdie said. "I have big news."

8

A Dark and Stormy Night

Did Birdie know about Dot and Dash? Or about Doc? Amelia couldn't think of what other big news there might be. Even so, her stomach folded in on itself. In her experience, news wasn't always a good thing.

Birdie sounded breathless. "The dragonfly staff is missing."

That *was* big news. Amelia shuddered. "Did somebody take it?"

"Nobody knows for sure," Birdie said.

"What an awful thing," Amelia said. "Will there be an article about it in the paper tomorrow?"

"Yup, and yours truly took the photo. It's of Mayor Hoffman standing next to Glenda the Sasquatch looking sad."

"Glenda looks sad now?" Amelia asked.

"No, Mayor Hoffman. But she was kind of faking it for the picture. She seems more mad than sad. Some of the things she said were unfit to print."

"Do you have any idea who did it?" Amelia said.

"No," Birdie said. "But my mom and dad think it's going to mess up the festival. A whole lot of people come for a swing of luck. It raises most of the Urchin Beach infrastructure budget. And you know better than anyone how much tourists spend at the shops that day."

"What are you saying?" Amelia asked. "Spell it out for me."

"The festival will be a bust, and Urchin Beach might go bankrupt," Birdie said. She didn't even sound scared or sick to her stomach. Amelia supposed it was because bad news was good for newspapers.

"Is Officer Locke going to open an investigation?" Amelia asked.

"My mom doesn't think so," Birdie said. "But that is her opinion." Birdie was always careful to separate opinions from facts that could be verified. It was her habit as a future journalist. "Officer Locke has a theory that the staff might have blown away."

"But it wasn't that windy," Amelia said. "I was watching the storm from the turret."

There was a silence, and Amelia knew Birdie was shrugging.

A thought took shape. "What if we solve it? We could act like detectives."

"I can't be a part of the story," Birdie said. "It's not what journalists do."

"Okay." Amelia knew better than to try to change Birdie's mind. Birdie took the rules of journalism seriously. It was one of Amelia's favorite things about her, even as she sometimes felt a twinge of envy that Birdie had clear rules to help her make decisions.

But solving the mystery was what Amelia wanted, even as it scared her. She wanted to be a part of the story—and not a bit part. She wanted to play a main role. She wanted to make a difference for her family and her community. She might even want this as much as she wanted Doc.

"I have news for you too," Amelia said.

"Tell me everything."

Amelia knew exactly what Birdie was doing. Leaning forward on her elbows, listening with her whole body. Amelia brought her up to speed on the Morse family. The inside of their creepy house. Kelly's fondness for sticks.

"The staff is a stick," Birdie said. "A specific kind of stick, but a stick nonetheless."

"Do you think she stole it?" Amelia asked.

Birdie exhaled and it made the sound of the ocean. "I can't speculate. You know that. But if someone were to investigate and then share their findings with the newspaper, well, I could spill ink for that."

"That's not all," Amelia said. "We got a dog."

"You buried the lede!" Birdie shouted. Amelia knew that was how journalists said you saved the most important stuff for last. "Good job, bestie. How'd you change your mom's and dad's minds?"

"With math," Amelia said. "Fractions, actually."

Birdie laughed. "Math turns out to be useful after all," she said. "Let's talk tomorrow. Tell me if you learn anything about the staff. And tell me what you think of my photo! I need feedback to get better!"

Bedtime came. The twins were in their cribs with their blanket halves. Colin had taken Doc to his room because he was the only one who didn't have anyone to share with. By the time Amelia and Bridget were safely in their bunks, the rain was still falling in buckets, but not the kind that make good housewarming gifts. What's more, a fierce wind had kicked in.

Amelia had long thought of wind as the rudest element. It was always pushing its way inside, making the air chilly, rustling papers on desks, even making the house creak. Wind wanted to be noticed. It wanted to make a person uncomfortable, both in body and spirit. That's bad manners, even for weather.

"Are you asleep?" Amelia asked.

"Yes." Bridget cracked up. She was a regular comedian.

Amelia, who slept in the top bunk, stared at the ceiling. It was easier to ask hard questions when you couldn't see the other person's face. "Are you worried about the staff?"

"Nope," Bridget said. "Someone probably knocked it off accidentally. Come to think of it, they've probably already found it."

"What if they haven't?" Amelia squinted. It was hard to tell in the dark, but it looked as though a new crack had formed in the ceiling. What if the house collapsed?

"They can get a new staff," Bridget said.

"But that one won't be the same," Amelia said. "It might not be lucky."

"It might be even luckier," Bridget said. "It might make people poop gold." She laughed.

"Do you want to help me solve the mystery?" Amelia asked.

"I can offer you a solid maybe," Bridget said. "I like to follow my passions, and if one of them strikes, I don't think I'll be able to resist. Sorry."

Amelia considered how strange it was that you could be in the same room as someone and still feel completely alone.

As she lay in her bunk, lightning flashed. Seconds later came a boom loud enough to rattle the windows.

Yarp, someone said. It sounded like Doc.

Then Colin came running in with Doc by his side.

"Uhhh," Colin said, "Doc is scared of storms. Can we sleep in here?"

"*Doc* is scared?" Bridget said. "More like *you* are, I bet."

"I'll help you pull out the trundle," Amelia said.

She climbed down. Bridget helped too, and before long, Colin and Doc were safely in the extra bed. Amelia and Bridget sat on the edge of Bridget's bunk and stroked Doc's silky ears and said soothing things.

"He's a really good dog," Amelia said.

"He's perfect," Bridget said.

"I wonder if he belongs to anyone," Colin said.

"He belongs to us, obviously." Bridget buried her face in Doc's fur. "Don't you, boy."

Amelia sighed. Bridget could say that all she wanted. But it didn't make it true. If her parents held firm on the no-dog rule, even though Doc was technically less than an entire dog, there was nothing they could do. She hated not knowing what was going to happen.

"Today was his lucky day," Colin said. "If we hadn't brought him in, he'd be out there in that storm."

Lucky. The mention of that word nudged Amelia's mind back to the missing staff. What if the missing staff had made Doc homeless?

What if its loss had brought the storm? There was another crack of lightning and thunder.

And then the power went out.

Amelia and Bridget climbed under the covers with Colin and Doc. The trundle bed was crowded, but Amelia didn't care.

"I'm scared," Colin said.

"You're hogging the blankets," Bridget said.

"We have to solve the mystery of the missing staff," Amelia said. "It's the only way to make things right again."

"You're not going to let that go, are you?" Bridget asked.

"I can't," Amelia said.

"Isn't that something that grown-ups are supposed to do?" Colin said.

"Usually, I guess," Amelia said. Part of her agreed with Colin. But part of her also wanted to see if she could crack the case. Not by herself. That seemed impossible. But with help from her siblings.

"If you do this, you're going to need to find clues," Bridget said. "And suspects. You'll probably need hats."

Amelia disagreed with that last part. Bridget always wanted hats. But she was right about clues and suspects.

"I already have some suspects," Amelia said.

"Who?" Colin asked.

"Not the Morses," Bridget said. "Tell me you don't suspect the new kids in town. Or their moms."

Leave it to Bridget to know that Amelia *did* suspect them—not that she was going to admit it now. Kelly had talked about how sticks were the only thing better than a bucket. She might have seen the staff and decided she had to have it. It was a possibility, no matter what Bridget thought. Or Jiera could have done it, knowing how much Kelly loved sticks. It could have been a crime of passion.

"Let's talk about it in the morning," Colin said. "We can't do anything here in the dark but wait for the storm to pass."

A sickening flash, and an even closer boom. The storm was right on top of them. Doc whined, and Amelia knew exactly how he felt.

URCHIN BEACH DRAGONFLY STAFF MISSING

Shocked Mayor Discovers the Crime, Wind Suspected

by Paula Wheeler, Editor in Chief

Sometime during Saturday morning's rainstorm, Urchin Beach's famous dragonfly staff disappeared from its location outside the town hall. Was it stolen? Did it blow away? Citizens are divided.

Urchin Beach mayor Miranda Hoffman discovered the loss late Saturday when she was inspecting the village for storm damage.

"I thought, worst-case scenario, I'd find downed branches or maybe some wet baby raccoons to look after," Mayor Hoffman said. "I am going to have to revise my definition of worst-case scenario because this is it."

It's the first time in the hundred-year history of Urchin Beach that the staff has been removed without authorization from the muscular wooden arms of Glenda, the nine-foot Sasquatch sculpture that serves as both a display and town mascot.

Hoffman said that without the lucky dragonfly staff, the town will have a hard time attracting tourists to the Dragonfly Day Festival taking place six days from now. Without tourists, the town businesses will be hard hit, and some might be forced to close their doors. Bankruptcy is also possible.

"But that would be a disaster," Mayor Hoffman said.

Local Realtor Mike Jung, a frequent critic of Hoffman, said, "How many times have I told that woman that a wooden Sasquatch is insufficient security for something as important as the dragonfly staff? At least eleven times, by my count. And that is a lot."

When this reporter told Mayor Hoffman what Jung had said, Hoffman fired back. "The town of Urchin Beach has always operated on trust and openness. We take pride in having one of the largest Sasquatch sculptures of any town, and Glenda has done a fine job of holding the staff for many years. Also, eleven isn't necessarily a lot. It's a lot if it's fingers, but it's not a lot if it's brain cells, which Mr. Jung has personal experience with."

"If I have eleven brain cells, she has four and a half," Jung replied.

Mayor Hoffman said that Urchin Beach security officer Shirley Locke was looking into the disappearance and had not yet ruled it a crime.

Locke said, "For all we know, a strong wind picked it up and carried it to the beach or some other nearby location. We need to keep our eyes peeled. It'll turn up."

"If that dragonfly staff stays missing," Jung said, "it could spell the end of life in Urchin Beach as we know it. Mark my words. This is a dog-gone catastrophe."

9

The Aftermath

By the time the sun rose the next morning, the damage from the storm had become clear. There was an article about it in the *Urchin Beach Gazette*, as well as one about the missing dragonfly staff. Birdie had done a good job taking pictures. She'd snapped shots of downed branches and got one of foamy rivulets of water rushing along the edge of the street.

Amelia called Birdie to congratulate her on her work and to see if her friend wanted to come over. But Birdie was busy.

"This is a big news weekend," she said.

It was just as well. The storm had not spared the MacGuffin house. The turret had sprung several leaks. That was the sort of thing that happened in a very rainy storm, and that kind of storm had become more common. Her parents talked about it all the time—and how important it was to take better care of the planet. Amelia agreed but could not help but feel worried every time the subject came up.

"Amelia! Bridget! Colin!" their mother shouted. "Bucket squad!"

The MacGuffins were not wealthy people. But they were rich in children and buckets. The three eldest MacGuffin kids placed buckets below the leaks. Then everyone went to the kitchen, where Mr. MacGuffin had made stacks of chocolate chip pancakes, his specialty. He had what Bridget called epic bedhead, and Amelia could tell he had a lot on his mind.

Still. He'd put a chocolate-free pancake on a plate for Doc, who sniffed it cautiously.

"It's okay," Mr. MacGuffin said. "Guests eat first."

"Doc isn't a guest," Bridget said. "He's family."

Amelia caught the look that passed between her parents. It was not a look that said, *We are so glad this long-lost family member made his way home.*

"About that," Mrs. MacGuffin said.

"We have to do things the right way," Mr. MacGuffin said.

"And then we can keep him?" Colin clasped his hands over his heart. His face had a pinched expression. How could her parents say no to that?

Mrs. MacGuffin sighed and checked her watch. "We have to take him to the vet. They're not open yet. But he needs to be examined, and they need to see if he has a microchip."

"What if he does?" Colin asked.

"If he has one, that will lead us to his owner."

"Oh," Colin said.

"Is it like a detective tool?" Amelia asked. She imagined the vet waving a wand over Doc's back and the chip beeping out a signal like she'd seen on television.

"Sort of," Mr. MacGuffin said. "They have information encoded in them. A name, a phone number, an address. We should be able to reach Doc's owner. I'm sure they miss him. He's a great dog."

"If he *has* owners," Bridget said. "He might not have a chip."

"Then we make flyers," Mrs. MacGuffin said. "We have to exhaust every possibility. We can't even think about taking him in yet."

"It's too late," Bridget said. "I've already been thinking about it."

Mr. and Mrs. MacGuffin laughed. Amelia didn't see what her parents thought was so funny. They'd *all* been thinking about keeping Doc. Obviously.

"What about the town staff?" she asked. "Is there any news on that?"

Mr. MacGuffin shook his head. "Surely we'll find it."

Amelia started. How did her dad know she was already on the case?

Then Mrs. MacGuffin spoke. "She will, kids. Shirley is a terrific security officer. And in the meantime, we can all focus on getting ready for Dragonfly Day."

Amelia sank in her chair. She'd misheard. Her dad had said, *Shirley will find it*, not, *Surely we'll find it*. She felt deflated.

"Come on, kids," Mr. MacGuffin said. "Why the long faces? You look like a bunch of horses." He waited for laughter that didn't come. "See, it's funny because horses have long faces."

"This isn't a time for jokes, Dad," Bridget said. "A dog's fate is in your hands."

"And the town has lost its lucky staff," Amelia said.

Mr. MacGuffin shrugged. "Don't worry about the staff, kids. This is a town full of love, and when you have that, you have all the luck that you need."

Mrs. MacGuffin looked at her watch again. "Let's team up," she said. "Dad needs someone to help him open the store. Everybody who wants to go with me to the vet, raise your hand."

All the MacGuffin children raised their hands. Amelia knew the twins didn't even understand why they were doing it. But she also knew they'd be no help to Dad. Much as she wanted to solve the mystery of whether Doc had owners, she lowered her hand.

"I'll help open the store," she said.

The neighborhood was drying out beneath a sky so blue it seemed incapable of having caused such a mess. People picked up branches and swept debris from the paths, and a chain saw screamed through the trunks of a fallen tree blocking the road.

Amelia and her father walked side by side to the Pacific General Store, their galoshes crunching on the damp oyster shell paths. When she was little, they used to hold hands on this trip. Much as she wanted to, she was too old for that now. Also, she doubted detectives held hands with their parents.

"The library," she said.

"Pardon me?" her father asked.

She hadn't meant to speak out loud, but the idea had come to her with such swiftness and certainty that it leapt out of her mouth like a frog. Their library had an extensive collection of nonfiction. Surely there was a book on being a detective. She could find out, if only she didn't have to help Mr. MacGuffin.

"Oh, nothing," she said.

"It sounded like you said 'the library,'" Mr. MacGuffin said.

"I did." There was no sense in denying it.

"Did you want to go?" he asked. "Because you could, if you'd like, after we get the store opened."

She squeezed her hands into fists and gave a little hop.

"I'll take that as a yes," her father said. "I'd love it if you got me the latest Linda Urban book."

"Of course." Her father loved Linda Urban even though her books were written for kids. Amelia hoped she would grow up to be the kind of grown-up who remembered that kids know what's good and not boring.

"What are you getting? Another Kekla Magoon? A William Alexander?"

"Probably," she said. And who knows, she might bring one home. He didn't know she was going to check out a book about being a detective. If she was efficient, she'd have it home and tucked away before everyone else got back from the vet. She didn't think her parents would try to talk her out of solving the mystery, but she also didn't want to take any chances. Nor did she want anyone to tease her about it. She hated teasing.

The Pacific General Store wasn't far from the town square. Amelia craned her neck to see if she could spot the staff. It wasn't there, of course. Only Glenda was, looking naked without it. In truth, even *with* it, Glenda was naked. You couldn't see anything beneath the carved fur, but the dragonfly staff had at least given her dignity.

"Who do you think took it, Dad?"

"Hmm?" He looked down at her. "Oh, the staff. Probably some kids doing a prank. It'll turn up."

He might be right, she thought. But none of the kids who lived in Urchin Beach would do such a thing. They all knew better. Most were gone at camp, like Delphine. And anyway, why now? Why right before the festival? Only someone who wanted to hurt the town would do that, and everyone who lived in Urchin Beach loved it.

Right?

Mr. MacGuffin pulled his key ring out of his pocket before they even reached the store. Already, a small line of sleepy-looking people had formed.

One of them was Mr. King, her third-grade teacher, who raised a fist in triumph when he saw them. "Our saviors are here!"

Mr. King's beard was longer than ever. Amelia had always liked being in his class because he would store pencils and other things there. She liked funny teachers. And she liked how she got to be one of the saviors, not just her dad. That was another good thing about him as a teacher: He saw kids as whole, entire people. They weren't just nubs.

"Hi, Mr. King," Amelia said.

"Still reading up a storm?" Mr. King said.

She nodded.

"Speaking of storms, last night was a doozy, eh, Dave?" Mr. King asked. "What did we do to deserve such lousy luck?"

Amelia knew the answer. It was the dragonfly staff.

"Beats me, Jerry." Mr. MacGuffin turned the key in the lock and pushed open the door. The bell rang merrily, but Amelia couldn't muster the excited feeling she usually got from the first ding of the day.

"Amelia here will help you all find what you need," Mr. MacGuffin said. "I'll get the store's brain up and running." The brain was the tablet they used to process payments. They used to have a cash register, but now it was in the storeroom, and it was only used by the MacGuffin kids when they were playing.

Almost everyone was there for buckets and cleaning supplies, and Amelia helped get her neighbors set. After the initial rush, it was quiet.

"Do you want me to dust?" Amelia asked.

"Your mom would love that," Mr. MacGuffin said. "You know her and dust."

Amelia did. It was the sort of thing her mother noticed and no one else did, but she was always so happy when everything in the general store sparkled. Amelia decided to start in her favorite section: puzzles, comics, and games.

"May I have some gum?" she asked.

"Sure thing," Mr. MacGuffin said.

She slipped a piece into her mouth, saving the tinfoil and paper wrapper, one to wrap the chewed gum in and one for some origami. As she chewed, she ran a dustcloth along the edges of the boxes, thinking about how strange it was that "dust" was both the stuff that collected on surfaces and the word for removing it. It was a contronym, a word that could also mean its opposite. How did such a thing happen? Why wasn't the word *undust*? Did the people who made up the word way back whenever have an argument over it, and did they say, "Fine. It's a tie"?

She wished she had someone to talk with about the mystery of words. Delphine was more likely to talk about TV shows or mantis shrimps. Birdie was more interested in photography. Bridget would shrug at contronyms and tell her to *watch me do a backflip*. Colin would do his best, but he was better with his hands than with his head and always needed Amelia to explain what she was thinking until her explanations started to feel weird in her mouth. The twins, well. Anything longer than a syllable was more than they could handle. No matter who she was with, part of Amelia always felt lonely.

Behind her, Mr. MacGuffin whistled.

"You are a heck of a duster," he said. "Top-notch. The best buster of dust, and dust we must. We must remove the dust."

"Dad," Amelia said.

He gave her a grin that she supposed was sheepish, although she'd never seen an actual sheep smile and couldn't be sure.

"I need you to do two teeny, tiny errands for me," he said. "And then you can go to the library."

She beamed as he handed her two buckets, one for Bonnie at the yarn shop and another for Clyde at the grocery store.

"Stay out of trouble!" he hollered.

"I will if you will!"

10

The First Clue

Amelia headed two doors down to Pins and Needles, Urchin Beach's yarn shop.

Bonnie clapped when she saw Amelia. "Oh, bless you, child."

Amelia handed her the bucket, and Bonnie dug in and pulled out fresh putty and a knife. "This old window. She's mostly made of leaks now."

Amelia felt sorry for the window. It was one of her favorites in town, made of dozens of little square panes. On sunny days, it shined like a jewel.

"Who's the other bucket for?" Bonnie asked.

"Grocery store," Amelia said.

"For Clyde?"

Amelia blushed on Bonnie's behalf. And for Clyde too. Everyone in town knew they had crushes on each other. But they never did anything about it.

"I should probably get it to him," Amelia said.

"I could bring it," Bonnie said.

Amelia considered the offer. But what if Bonnie didn't deliver? What if she kept the bucket? What if she was a thief and she also had the dragonfly staff? Amelia looked around the shop, her gaze settling on the cubbies of wooden knitting needles. The staff would blend right in. Granted, it would be much bigger, like the size of a novelty knitting needle. At this stage of her investigation, she couldn't rule anything out.

"Well?" Bonnie asked.

Amelia saw no sign of the staff in the shop. But giving Bonnie a chance to blink her eyelashes at Clyde wasn't Amelia's job. Bringing him a bucket was.

"It's all right," she said. "I've got it."

She went around the corner to the Crab 'N' Go, where Clyde had pulled his wheelchair up to a display and was arranging lettuce in a wooden bin. He had a knack for it. He'd made a face out of different-colored lettuces and used onions for eyes. It was neat, but she couldn't see what Bonnie saw in him. He was Clyde. He was about as romantic as a tuna.

"Hello, Amelia. Do you know how to tell if a pineapple is ripe?" He hung the bucket over a hook on the side of his chair.

"Yes." He'd given her frequent instructions on how to tell if every sort of imaginable fruit was ready for eating.

"Oh." He looked disappointed.

"But you can remind me," Amelia said. "I might have it confused with, um, avocados."

"That's a strange thing to have confused," Clyde said. "Here. Let me show you an avocado and a pineapple together, so you can see how different they are."

Amelia wanted to say that she *knew* the difference between the two, but he looked so excited that she kept her mouth shut. Before long, Clyde finished. He thanked Amelia for the bucket, which contained duct tape, a hammer, and nails, and he gave her a juicy plum to eat on her way to the library. It looked delicious. She spat out her gum, wrapped it in foil, and dropped it into Clyde's trash.

The library wasn't far. As she bit into the plum, she passed beneath the countdown to Dragonfly Day sign. Someone had put up the number six. Six days left to solve the mystery. The plum, which had tasted so sweet, became sour in her mouth. She dropped the pit in the compost section of the trash receptacle on the corner.

Amelia couldn't bring herself to go inside the library yet. She wanted to check the scene of the crime for clues. She didn't know much about being a detective, but she knew that was the first thing they did, and she was late to do that. She also knew that criminals often returned to the scene of the crime. It made her nervous to think about coming face-to-face with a thief. Then again, if the thief did return, she could catch them.

The town hall was a few yards ahead. She approached it as if she hadn't a care in the world, in case the thief was watching. As soon as she reached Glenda, she'd turn around and pretend she was merely taking in the lovely Urchin Beach scenery.

She reached the Sasquatch, turned, and scanned the sidewalk and street. No one was there. Not even a squirrel. So much for an easy collar.

Amelia studied Glenda. Maybe it *would* have been smart to keep the staff locked up instead of leaving it in the arms of a giant outdoor Sasquatch statue. But she understood Mayor Hoffman's point of view. What's more, she respected the mayor's judgment. She was one of only two Black mayors in the state. In a country where there had been laws that disadvantaged Black people, the mayor's accomplishments were even more impressive.

Amelia examined the ground around Glenda. She could see indentations in the damp grass, but nothing that said, *I am the footstep of a thief.* A smear of mud marred the white wooden platform where Glenda stood, but anyone could have left that. Anyone or anything.

She scrutinized the streak, and that's when she noticed something peculiar. She scraped it, and sure enough, a hair came loose. A red hair, straight and wiry. It was the length of, say, Dash's hair. Or Dot's bangs. No one else in town had hair that color. A red-haired tourist could have left it behind, she reasoned. But what tourist would have been out in the previous day's rainstorm?

Lucky thing she had the gum wrapper. She folded the strand of hair inside and stowed the clue in her pocket. She would have to get a sample from one of the Morse kids and see if it matched. That was going to be tricky.

Miss Fortune looked up from the reference desk at the library with a wide smile.

"Well, if it isn't the biggest MacGuffin!"

This wasn't technically accurate. Both her father and mother were MacGuffins of larger size. But Miss Fortune meant well. And Amelia *was* the biggest of the MacGuffin offspring.

"How can I help?" Miss Fortune rested her chin on her hands.

Amelia asked about the Kekla Magoon, William Alexander, and Linda Urban titles.

"Excellent choices. Olugbemisola Rhuday-Perkovich and Kelly Barnhill also have new books that you'd like. And maybe an Anne Ursu for Colin? Laurel Snyder? Laura Ruby? Or wait—Tracey Baptiste?"

"Okay," Amelia said. "One of each." She was wishing she'd brought a backpack. Or a bucket. This was starting to sound heavy. "But I also need nonfiction."

Miss Fortune snapped up and rubbed her palms together. "Kate Messner?"

"Has she written anything about being a detective?"

Miss Fortune cocked her head. "I don't think so. I can think of lots of mysteries written for kids, though. Sheela Chari is a wonderful author."

"I need a book that will teach me how to solve a crime."

Miss Fortune narrowed her eyebrows. "Are you thinking about the dragonfly staff?"

Amelia braced herself. Miss Fortune was probably going to tell her that books like that were not for kids. But that's not what happened. Miss Fortune tapped her top lip a few times. She squinted and stared into space. Then she clicked at the library keyboard, scrolled through the results, looked at Amelia, and said, "Follow me."

Miss Fortune led her to some stacks in the back of the library.

"Dewey decimal section 153," she said. "Conscious mental processes and intelligence."

Amelia liked the sound of that. Miss Fortune crouched and removed a volume from the shelf. She blew on the book, and a puff of dust emerged. She held the volume out to Amelia. *How to Think Like a Master Detective* by Edith Phipps, PhD.

"Her other book is about cats," Miss Fortune said. "So I don't think it would be of much use here."

Amelia agreed.

"But, you know," Miss Fortune said, "you do live next door to one of the world's finest mystery writers. If anyone could teach you how to be a detective, it would be Dr. Agatha."

Amelia wanted detective lessons from Dr. Agatha about as much as she wanted a fly to lay an egg beneath her skin. About as much as she wanted that egg to hatch. About as much as she wanted the larva to climb out and say, "Greetings and salutations."

"Great idea," she said.

"Is there something wrong with your mouth?" Miss Fortune said.

"This is how I smile," Amelia said.

"Oh." Miss Fortune scanned the shelves again. "Well, I think that book will be a good place for you to start. Get your little gray cells shipshape."

Amelia knew it was only her imagination, but the red hair in her pocket felt alive and urgent. As if it had something to tell her. As soon as she could, she planned to take it out, study it, and use her detective book to unravel its secrets. And she'd get help from her siblings because this was not something she could do on her own.

11

Thinking Like a Master Detective

The house was quiet. Mrs. MacGuffin and the rest of the family had not yet returned from the vet. Was that a good sign or a bad one? Amelia called Birdie's cell phone from the landline in the kitchen, but Birdie didn't pick up. A busy news day, maybe, although sometimes, when Birdie didn't answer, Amelia wondered whether she wanted to be friends anymore. Birdie always said Amelia was being a worrywart—that they were forever friends. But how could she be certain?

Amelia sat at the kitchen table, took a deep breath, and cracked open *How to Think Like a Master Detective*. She doubted it would have any information on solving a mystery as small as what had happened with Doc at the vet's, or as personal as the state of her friendship with Birdie. She'd never really thought about how many mysteries there were in the world before this. But now it felt as if they were everywhere. Small ones. Personal ones. Mysteries that could change the fate of an entire town.

She evened off a rough fingernail with her teeth. If the book did solve the mystery of Doc, what would she do if she didn't like the answer? Already, the house looked like a place where a dog lived. Where a dog belonged. There were muddy paw prints by the back door and two bowls on the floor, one for food and one for water. Someone had also found a rubber ball that looked as if it wanted to be thrown. All this evidence of Doc's presence gave Amelia a pang. She did not want to have to give him up. She would if he belonged to another family, of course. She would have to, but it would be excruciating.

The grandfather clock in the hall ticked, reminding her that she had a bigger mystery to solve and not much time to do it: Who had stolen the dragonfly staff? She found her courage, stopped chewing her fingernail, and scanned the table of contents. *Equipment. Mindset. Surveillance. Deduction. The Art of Disguise. Lock Picking.*

Solving a crime looked complicated. She ran a finger down the page and stopped at a chapter called "Evidence." She turned to it.

There are many types of evidence that a crime or crimes have been committed, the chapter began. *It's not all blood spatters and fingerprints.*

Amelia was relieved. Blood belonged inside bodies. End of story. Once it came out—gross.

As the clock ticked away, Amelia read. Hair samples were a legitimate clue after all. She reached into her pocket and set the folded gum wrapper on the table. Carefully she opened it.

She didn't have access to a lab that would help her analyze the DNA of the hair. But the book said the clue would speak to her.

Clues can whisper. They can speak in a proper indoor voice. Sometimes, Edith Phipps, PhD, wrote, *they can shout.*

She heard this clue loud and clear. Whose hair could it be but one of the Morse twins? They were her prime suspects. They had to be. She listed the reasons:

- They were kids, and her dad had said kids were the most likely culprits.
- The staff had disappeared the very day they arrived.
- Kelly Morse had admitted to liking sticks. Most likely Dot and Dash did too.

Amelia's shoulders drooped. Even though Dot and Dash were seventh graders, they seemed nice. They'd been friendly and welcoming. They also knew a secret code, one she very much wished to learn.

If they hadn't been criminals as well as seventh graders, Amelia would have hoped to be friends.

She sat back in her chair, reasonably certain she'd solved the crime. The book had been useful, although she was disappointed that she wouldn't get to pick any locks. That looked fun. Colin was *really* going to like that chapter, which came with instructions on how to construct a device for lock picking.

What was the next step? An accusation, she supposed. Bridget would be good at that part—if she was willing to make one. They could bring Dot and Dash to justice as a family and then restore the stolen staff to its rightful place.

The book had no chapter about the justice part of mystery solving. She couldn't help but feel a bit disappointed in Edith Phipps, PhD. Amelia flipped to the back of the book and looked at the picture of the author. An older lady, sort of like Dr. Agatha but less muscular. She'd posed in front of an oil painting of a cat.

Amelia resumed chewing her fingernail and thought about how it felt to be a detective. Pretty good, actually. It called on many of her strengths. She was smart. She was observant. But she'd also been afraid, and she was surprised to realize that her fear had been useful. It had given her a reason to solve the case: Without the staff, Urchin Beach would suffer. Her parents' store would suffer, which meant finances at the MacGuffin house would be even tighter than usual. A tighter budget meant no dog for sure. That was a big part of her motive for solving the crime. And she'd done it using the best and worst parts of her. Maybe she was cut out for this work after all.

There was a scraping sound. A key in the lock. And then the voices of her mom and siblings—along with the scrabbling of dog toenails.

She folded the hair back into the wrapper and then tucked both inside the library book. She'd read more later in case there were other crimes to solve. There was no doubt lots of good stuff she'd missed. Then she sprang out of her chair and hurried to the door.

"What did the veterinarian say?"

"Can you help me with the twins?" Mrs. MacGuffin pushed her bangs out of her eyes. Colin and Bridget crouched by Doc, scratching his ears. Amelia wanted to do that too, and she wanted to tell them the progress she'd made solving the crime. But those things could wait.

"Sure, Mom," she said.

Her mom scooped up Duncan. Amelia held Emma's chubby hand. They climbed the stairs to the twins' bedroom, which was across the hall from hers.

It wasn't easy to change the diapers of twin toddlers. Amelia understood why her mother wanted help. As she sealed Emma's diaper cover, she asked about Doc.

"Did he . . . did he have a chip?"

Her mother exhaled hard. "He did."

Amelia's chest tightened. "Oh."

"It's more complicated than that, though," Mrs. MacGuffin said. "Let's make lunch and I'll explain."

12

Grilled Cheese and Suspects

"This seems like a grilled-cheese-and-tomato-soup kind of day, doesn't it?" Mrs. MacGuffin asked.

Amelia thought every day could be a grilled-cheese-and-tomato-soup kind of day. Mr. MacGuffin always baked challah on Fridays, and it made excellent grilled cheese. Soft and crispy, the perfect complement to gooey cheese and tangy soup.

As Mrs. MacGuffin heated chopped onions in melted butter, Amelia sliced bread and cheese for the sandwiches.

"Doc had a microchip," Mrs. MacGuffin said, "but when the vet called the number, it had been disconnected. We could have left him at the vet's, but they'd have to send him to a shelter. It seemed kinder to bring him here. The vet had the address on the file, and they'll mail the family a letter."

"And then what will happen?" Amelia asked.

"That will be their official notification that Doc's been found," her mother said. "If the owners don't respond—"

"Then he's ours?"

There was a long stretch during which Mrs. MacGuffin didn't reply as she stirred tomatoes and broth into the pot. When she spoke, her voice sounded tired. "It's not that simple."

It seemed simple to Amelia. Doc needed a home. They needed a dog. The end. Maybe he would be so healthy he'd never need to go to the vet. Or maybe Amelia could get some sort of job.

"I'll want to visit the address myself," her mother said. "If they're not there, we could see if they left a forwarding address. Sometimes dogs get lost in accidents or when people move houses. If he was your dog, wouldn't you want the person who found him to make every attempt to return him?"

Amelia nodded. But it was hard to think about Doc that way. It was a lot easier to think the people he belonged to first hadn't cared, wouldn't care, didn't want him. It made it hard to know what to hope for—Doc getting his old family back, or their family getting to keep him.

"Can I go with you when you do?" she asked.

"Of course," Mrs. MacGuffin said.

Mrs. MacGuffin kept stirring while Amelia put a pan on a burner for the sandwiches. "What are our new neighbors like?" Mrs. MacGuffin asked. "Did they enjoy their bucket?"

Bridget barged in holding Emma, who held her half blanket. "Everyone enjoys buckets."

"Bucket. Want bucket," Emma said.

"There are two kids, Dot and Dash," Bridget said. "Zero pets that I saw, but I didn't get to look in the boxes or go into any bedrooms, and they could have hamsters or pythons or something. And two moms, but I forget their names."

"Kelly and Jiera." Amelia felt uncomfortable. If Dot and Dash were thieves, their mothers might be criminal masterminds. They didn't seem that way, but if they were extremely evil, then seeming normal would be a brilliant disguise.

"What's that look on your face mean, Amelia?" Mrs. MacGuffin asked.

"It means she is thinking something that she doesn't want to say." Bridget shifted Emma to her other hip.

Amelia wished Bridget wouldn't read her mind. If it's happening inside your head, it should be private. That's the whole point of having a skull. It's closed. Like a door.

To prove Bridget wrong even though she had been right, Amelia said, "I think the Morse twins stole the dragonfly staff."

"I knew it!" Bridget said.

Mrs. MacGuffin raised an eyebrow. "What makes you say that?"

"Yeah," Bridget said. "They didn't look like thieves."

"How do thieves look?" Amelia said. "And how would you know, anyway?"

"I've watched TV," Bridget said. "I know things."

Mrs. MacGuffin laughed. "When I was a kid there was a thief named the Hamburglar, and he wore stripes and a mask."

"For real?" Bridget said.

"He was a character in a commercial. But he did have that costume."

Amelia felt sorry for her mom. Only a sad child would watch commercials in the first place. And to remember them all these years later—what a waste of brain.

"They were probably good commercials, Amelia," Bridget said.

Bridget had done it again. Figured out what Amelia was thinking. Which meant she might be right about the Morse twins. It made Amelia feel like arguing.

"I found a clue," Amelia said. "Evidence. A red hair left behind at the scene of the crime." When she said it out loud, it didn't feel as certain as when she'd been sitting alone reading about evidence in her detective book.

Colin and Doc wandered in, with Duncan toddling behind them.

"When's lunch? We're hungry," Colin said.

Doc leaned against Colin's leg, his pink tongue hanging out. Duncan sat next to them and rested his head on Doc's shoulder.

Doc really was the best dog she'd ever seen.

"Amelia needs to flip the sandwiches," Mrs. MacGuffin said. "When they're nice and crispy, we eat. I'd like you to stop suspecting the neighbors of a crime, though. It's not the Urchin Beach way. And that hair could have come from anywhere."

"Blanket," Duncan said. "Want it."

Mrs. MacGuffin sighed audibly. "We'll find it after lunch, little bunbun." She scooped him up, and then they all sat at the kitchen table to eat.

13

Doc Needs a Walk

Lunch was delicious. They sipped their soup from the cobalt-blue mugs Mr. and Mrs. MacGuffin had received as a wedding gift. Soup was much more delicious in mugs, and the blue ones were perfect. Thick and solid and just the right size.

But by the end of the meal, Amelia felt unsatisfied. It wasn't that she was hungry. Her certainty that the Morse twins had stolen the staff had diminished. She wasn't sure what to do next: get a hair sample from their heads, or move on to the next suspect.

"All right, kids," Mrs. MacGuffin said after they washed up. "Doc needs a walk."

"Doc," Duncan said.

"Walk," Emma said.

"I get to hold the leash!" Bridget said.

"Awww," Colin said. "I'm going to invent a leash with five handles so we can all hold him. I know! I can use Dad's belts. He won't notice."

Colin ran back inside and returned, breathing heavily, with two belts. "I thought Dad had more," he said.

They clipped the belts and a new leash on Doc's collar, which was also new. Mrs. MacGuffin wouldn't have bought new things if there wasn't reason for hope, right? Amelia stuffed some bags in her pocket because Doc could not wear a diaper. Then the five of them set out, Amelia holding the leash and the twins holding the belts. Colin and Bridget each held a twin's hand.

Most of the puddles from the previous day's storm had drained away. The Morse twins were cruising down Sand Dollar Lane on their bicycles. Amelia pretended that she hadn't seen them. She felt awful that she'd been so certain of their guilt. She was afraid the Morse twins would take one look at her and know.

"Look!" Bridget shouted. "It's Dot and Dash!"

She pulled the line of MacGuffins toward them.

"WE GOT A DOG!" Bridget announced.

Dot and Dash backpedaled to stop, carving half circles in the street as they did. Amelia kept her face down as she approached.

"Nice dog," Dash said. "What's its name?"

"Doc," Colin said. "He was a stray."

"I have a question," Bridget said. "It's important."

Amelia blanched. Her mouth went dry. She knew what was coming.

"Did you guys take the town dragonfly staff? Amelia thinks you did."

"What's a dragonfly staff?" Dot asked.

"Every year we have the Dragonfly Day Festival," Colin said. "The staff is a sort of totem believed to bestow good luck on people who touch it."

"But you have to pay five dollars first," Bridget said. "Cash or charge."

Dash laughed.

"How do you know the staff was stolen?" Dot asked.

"Because it's not there anymore," Bridget said. "Someone would have had to take it. It wasn't the wind. There's been plenty of windier days."

Bridget was making good points, Amelia thought.

"Maybe someone is getting it cleaned up for that parade thing," Dash said. "Like, polishing it or something."

Amelia didn't like how the Morse twins were doubting that a

crime had even occurred. They might be innocent, but being contradictory was rude. And the Dragonfly Day Festival was a lot more than a parade. There was a whole celebration marking the emergence of dragonflies from the slough nestled between Urchin Beach, the highway, and the beach.

In addition to being the state insect, green darner dragonflies were an essential part of the ecosystem. Not only did they eat mosquitoes, but they also became food for fish and birds. And if the dragonflies were missing, it could mean that their water wasn't clean and healthy, so they were an important way to know whether the environment was in good shape.

"If someone was polishing it, the mayor would know," Bridget said. "That's part of her official duties."

Dash made a thoughtful face. "Sounds like it was stolen, then. But we didn't do it. We were busy all day moving, and we have our mothers as an alibi. Plus the movers. They'd vouch for us. I swear on a holy telegraph that we didn't go anywhere but from the moving truck to the house and back again. I don't even know where the staff was before it was taken. I read about it in the *Gazette*."

"Besides," Dot said, "thieves have to have a motive. What would our motive be?"

"Evidence too," Dash said. "There needs to be a motive, the

opportunity, and evidence. We didn't have the opportunity. We were moving. That's our alibi. We don't have a motive either, and you don't have evidence."

Amelia didn't want Dot and Dash to hate her. She *hoped* they might even like her. But who would like someone who accused people of a crime?

"Then how do you explain the red hair found at the scene of the crime?" Bridget asked. "Amelia found one. She showed us at lunch. Amelia, show them the hair."

Amelia swallowed hard. "I don't have it anymore." That wasn't true. It was still in the book. But she didn't want Dot and Dash to think she was a creep.

"I can see how that would look suspicious," Dash said. "You're a pretty good detective to have found evidence like that, Amelia."

Amelia felt relief from her toes to her scalp. And something more, something that made her face burn.

Dot looked thoughtful. "We didn't go anywhere near the statue. It's true that hair floats. But it might not even belong to one of us."

"You are the only redheads in town," Bridget said. "And it was raining. I don't think hair floats when it's raining."

"That seems like more of a windy-day thing," Colin said. "And it wasn't windy until night, and the staff was already stolen then."

Amelia wished Bridget and Colin would drop it.

"I'm sure it's nothing," she said. "Or a coincidence."

Dot said, "Well, it's a real shame about the staff."

Dash shrugged. "Are the police investigating?"

"There aren't police in Urchin Beach. Only Shirley Locke, our security officer. We call her Officer Locke, but grown-ups get to call her Shirl."

"Is she any good?" Dot asked.

"She's really nice," Colin said. "If you get locked out of your car, she'll open it for you. She also inflates bike tires and gives out lollipops. But there are never actual crimes in Urchin Beach, unless you count what raccoons do to trash cans, so she might be out of practice."

"Let's go talk to her," Dash said. "You've gotten me curious."

"Wouldn't you rather go look at the dragonfly habitat? I know a shortcut," Bridget said.

"Crime first," Dot said. "That's the main course. The habitat can be dessert."

Amelia liked the sound of group detecting, and Dot and Dash had offered up a convincing defense. She wasn't going to cross them off the suspect list entirely, but she had reason to doubt their guilt that she hadn't had before. Officer Locke might be able to help them zero

in on a new suspect.

Time was running out, though. The Dragonfly Day Festival was

six days off. That wasn't a lot of time to solve the crime of the cen-

tury in Urchin Beach.

14

The Thief Feels Lucky

The thief remained in Urchin Beach. The thief liked it there. The thief liked walking the oyster shell paths. The thief liked the way people offered greetings as they passed—well, all except that one gray-haired lady.

It hadn't always been this way for the thief, who'd time and time again endured the sting of rejection. Urchin Beach felt different. As if it might be a place to stay. A place to put down roots. A place to make friends.

For the first time, the thief felt lucky. If the thief had been told the dragonfly staff was a lucky object, the thief would have believed it. If the luck had been tomato soup, the thief's mug would have overflowed.

The thief strolled through Urchin Beach, looking at town hall. The library. The Pacific General Store. All the children. The tan-faced, red-haired twins. The brown-skinned girl with the camera and note-book. The family of five kids who looked the same, except for the one with glasses. The busy adults, many of them carrying buckets.

Yes, it was a very nice place.

As the thief walked, something wonderful came into view. A small thing. A child's toy, soft and colorful, though that's not why the thief wanted it. The thief wanted it because the thief was good at understanding what was valuable and what was vulnerable.

The toy was both.

The thief planned to return when the coast was clear.

That's when the thief would take it.

15

Officer Shirley Locke's Home Security Headquarters

Officer Shirley Locke's office was a van. She called it her mobile security headquarters.

"This means that wherever danger goes, I can be hot on its heels," she liked to say.

The van read SHIRLEY LOCKE'S HOME SECURITY and provided her phone number along with an email account "recommended for nonemergencies."

Amelia wondered whether they should have called first. The crime *felt* like an emergency, but it wasn't happening at that very moment. What made something an emergency? She hesitated in the shadow of the van, clutching Doc's leash as though it were a lifeline.

Dash strode to the sliding door on the van and knocked. *TAP-tap-tuh-TAP-TAP.*

The door slid open, as if by magic, but Amelia knew there was a button inside that Shirley Locke had pressed.

Officer Locke sat inside at a small desk. She held a phone to one ear, a walkie-talkie to the other, and a pen clamped between her teeth.

She said, "Ot ow, ids," but her meaning was clear: Not now, kids.

Then she spat out the pen, which landed softly on the desk. "Not you, Mayor Hoffman. I was talking with the MacGuffins, the dog they've secured with a leash and their father's belts, and"—she looked at the Morse twins—"a couple of red-haired seventh graders who are new in town. Tell me more about this emergency at the beach."

Amelia was impressed by Officer Locke's deductive skills. She'd gotten everything exactly right.

"What kind of emergency at the beach?" Bridget asked.

Officer Locke turned away from the children and Doc and toward a poster advertising the Wing Luke Museum in Seattle.

"How rude," Bridget muttered.

"Rude!" Duncan and Emma said, but in louder voices.

Officer Locke didn't seem to hear. She kept talking to the mayor on one phone and someone else on the walkie-talkie. "Yes. A total collapse. We'll need to reinforce the cliff, so whatever supplies you have. And wood. Buckets too."

Amelia narrowed her eyes. Buckets? Supplies? Officer Locke had to be talking with Mr. MacGuffin on the walkie-talkie. Whatever had happened at the beach required the input of both the mayor and Amelia's father. That was big. The kids exchanged glances that contained an entire unspoken dialogue.

What do you think happened?

I don't know. What do YOU think happened?

I don't know, which is why I asked.

Do you think we should check it out?

Definitely.

Do you think we'll get in trouble?

We can pretend we didn't know any better.

When should we go?

Now. Duh.

Doc's expression was also easy to read. *I'll go anywhere you go, and I would even go without this leash and these two belts.*

Dot Morse gently closed the door to Officer Locke's mobile security office. "Where's the beach?" she asked.

"Not far," Bridget said.

"We should take the twins home first," Amelia said.

"That will take too long," Bridget said.

"Do you think it will be safe for them?" Amelia asked.

"Don't be such a worrywart," Bridget said.

"They probably need new diapers," Colin said.

"Then you should probably go change them," Bridget said.

"No poop," Emma said.

"No pee," Duncan said.

Amelia wanted to stay on the case. She also wanted to make sure the twins weren't in any danger. This was hard.

"Come on, Amelia," Bridget said. "Once we're done with this, we can go check on the dragonfly nymphs. If anything happens to their habitat, that's way worse than a missing staff."

Amelia knew what Bridget was saying about the dragonfly nymphs. But maybe if the staff hadn't been stolen, the storm wouldn't have been as disastrous. And there wouldn't have been a collapse. It was all connected—and everything led back to the staff.

"The beach is this way," Amelia said to Dot and Dash. "Follow us."

Colin took Emma's hand. Bridget took Duncan's. Amelia held firmly to Doc's leash, while the twins gripped the belts. They headed west, toward the sea.

16

On Stiff Upper Lips

The trouble was monstrous. Amelia knew it the moment they reached the edge of town. Before the storm, a grove of Sitka spruce trees had separated the town from the beach itself. The trees grew on a high bluff, their stiff branches permanently blown sideways by daily breeze from the sea.

Amelia loved the trees. Their green froth of branches. Their molasses-cookie bark. The frills of lichen that hung from them, a pop of chartreuse that looked as if it had been left behind by partying gnomes. The trees also held the slope in place, keeping the pumpkin-colored bluff from crumbling onto the sand below.

Now several of the largest, oldest trees were gone. Ripped out, as if a giant hand had descended from the sky and tossed them aside. Their exposed roots looked like a nightmare version of their branches: twisted, filthy, and deeply wrong.

That wasn't all.

The wooden staircase that had once been anchored into the soil had collapsed. Its treads and railing littered the sand. The town needed the staircase. It was the only safe way to the beach. South of the staircase, there was a way to drive onto the sand, but that was just for people who couldn't use the stairs. The shoreline ecosystem was too fragile for more traffic than that. Without the staircase, there was effectively no beach access. And without access to the beach, there could be no real Dragonfly Day Festival. They'd have to do everything in town, which wouldn't be the same. It wouldn't be special. It wouldn't raise the money the town needed to survive. There might not even be a dragonfly sighting.

The MacGuffin children stood in a line holding hands, belts, and leash. Dot and Dash were next to them. At least half the town was there too. Bonnie. Clyde. Mr. King. Miss Fortune. Mr. Jung. A few kids who hadn't gone to camp: Hayden Murphy, Eugenides Turner, and Kat Bacon.

Birdie raced up with her hair in puffs, which was Amelia's favorite style. Birdie changed hairstyles all the time, as if it was no big deal. She wore a camera around her neck and carried a notebook, like a real reporter, which reminded Amelia to act like a real detective.

She scanned the crowd for suspects and narrowed her eyes at

Eugenides. In kindergarten, he'd stolen her tiny hamburger eraser and pretended it was his. He'd stolen several food-shaped erasers from classmates, it turned out—making him a real-life Hamburglar. Could Eugenides Turner be the thief? She'd have to consider his motive, opportunity, and any evidence that might turn up.

"Wow," Bridget said. "That is a mess."

"There's other beach access, right?" Dot asked.

"Not really. You *can* climb down the bluff," Bridget said, "but you need skills or a rope. It's gnarly."

"And we're not supposed to go near the bluff," Colin said. "If your car has a disabled placard, you are allowed to drive on the beach not too far from here. But the other beach access points are miles down the road, and at certain times of day, the water is too high to get here from there."

"High tide," Dash said.

He knew the ways of the sea, Amelia thought. Then she rolled her eyes at herself. *The ways of the sea.* Where did that even come from?

"Your face is really red," Bridget said. "Like a crab shell."

"No, it isn't." Amelia turned away and spotted a familiar figure. "Look, there's Dad!"

He was climbing down the bluff with a rope and a bucket over his shoulder.

The MacGuffin children looked in the direction Amelia was pointing. So did Doc and the Morse twins.

"I hope he doesn't get hurt," Clyde said.

"That's the last thing our town needs," Bonnie said. "An injured MacGuffin."

"What's he doing?" Colin said.

"This and that." Bridget flopped her hand back and forth. "Obviously."

Amelia watched a moment longer. "My guess is that he'll be examining the wreckage at the bottom and then deciding what can be done about it."

"There's nothing that *can* be done about it," a voice announced.

Amelia knew without looking who'd spoken. The voice sounded as if its owner had gargled rocks for years. Amelia held her siblings' hands tighter and stole a peek at Dr. Agatha. Surely the mystery writer and possible murderer wasn't talking to the MacGuffins. Not when so many people from the village had gathered by the shore. Surely she was talking to an adult.

"You there. The oldest MacGuffin. Ophelia." Dr. Agatha's voice was louder and more insistent.

"Me?" Amelia said.

"Yes, you. Ophelia."

"Her name is Amelia," Bridget said.

"That's what I said. Cordelia." And then she laughed. "I was pulling your leg. I know your name is Amelia. It was a test."

A test? Amelia did not much like tests.

"Don't look so crestfallen," Dr. Agatha said. "You passed the manners test, but not the forthrightness test. That, I have deduced, is your sister's area of expertise."

"I'm always right," Bridget said. "Forthright, fifthright. However many times it takes."

"You said there's nothing that can be done about it," Amelia said. "What do you mean by that?"

"I mean the stairs are gone. The slope is unstable. If it can be fixed, which is a mighty if, it will take a great deal of wherewithal, which is always in short supply and almost certainly not to be found before the festival. Which means the festival won't happen. Which means the town of Urchin Beach is cooked."

"Cooked?" Colin said.

"Cooked," Dr. Agatha said. "Like a goose, only there is no goose, no heat source, and no one will get dinner afterward."

"Could you say that again?" Birdie said. "I'm trying to get a quote for the paper, and you talk really fast."

Dr. Agatha stared at Birdie. She did not repeat herself. Birdie slowly stepped back until she was partially hidden behind a row of adults in the crowd. She put her camera in front of her face and snapped pictures. Amelia pressed her leash hand to her heart so Birdie would know Amelia was on her side.

The crowd murmured. Dr. Agatha was the oldest resident in the town. She was the most famous. The most eccentric. The most admired. The most feared. No one doubted her prediction.

"This is what happens," Dr. Agatha said. "Time marches on, and it tends to march past little places that are far from the center of everything."

"She's kind of a grump," Dot whispered.

Amelia nodded.

"But we can take a small measure of solace in this," Dr. Agatha said. "Tourists are a nuisance."

Amelia narrowed her eyes.

"They buy a lot of yarn," Bonnie said.

"And crab," Clyde said. "But to be honest, pineapples aren't all that popular. So much for it being a vacation fruit."

Hayden Murphy poked Eugenides in the back. Eugenides took a reluctant step forward. "Is Urchin Beach going to die? I mean, as a town?"

"Everything dies," Dr. Agatha said. "I'm sorry to report this, but it is true."

"That's not an appropriate thing to say in front of children," Mr. King said. "And I should know. I'm a teacher."

"Then you ought to be teaching them the facts of life," Dr. Agatha said.

Mr. King crossed his arms and muttered, "You don't need to say it with a hammer."

Kat Bacon began to weep.

"You there," Dr. Agatha said. "The girl with the rainbow braces. Stop crying. Moments like this call for a stiff upper lip."

Amelia concentrated on her own upper lip. It didn't feel stiff except when she made a duck face. She thought about the expression. Even if "stiff upper lip" wasn't literal, it made no sense. She'd seen sad babies. When babies cried, their *lower* lips experienced all the motion. If anything, *that* was the lip that should be kept stiff.

"It's because of the staff, isn't it," said Clyde.

"The staff is stuff and nonsense," Dr. Agatha said. "Superstition."

"Talk slower," Birdie said. "Please!"

"But the storm came *after* the staff was taken," said Mr. King.

"How do you know? Did you witness it?" Dr. Agatha asked. "Even so, correlation is not causation."

"What she's saying," Bridget said slowly, almost certainly for Birdie's sake, "is that it's a coincidence. We shouldn't get our T-shirts in a wad over it."

"You don't miss much, do you, second MacGuffin," Dr. Agatha said.

"I miss nothing," Bridget said. "I'm also freakishly flexible and strong. Watch this." She gave Duncan's chubby hand to Amelia and did a back walkover, right at the edge of the cliff. Amelia didn't necessarily agree with the argument that Bridget missed nothing. It was impressive, though, that she knew what Dr. Agatha was talking about. She was only an almost fifth grader, after all.

Amelia had also guessed Dr. Agatha's meaning, but she still planned to look up the words in her dictionary when she returned home, to be sure. That was maybe the big difference between her and Bridget. Amelia liked to make sure. Bridget was born sure.

Amelia felt a twinge of suspicion, first, at Mr. King. How did he know the storm came after the staff was taken—unless he'd taken it? Or, wait. What if Dr. Agatha had taken the staff? She seemed mean enough. She hated tourists. That was a motive, which Mr. King did not have. Did Dr. Agatha have the opportunity? Perhaps. All Amelia needed to do was confirm that and find some evidence. Then she could be sure she'd solved the crime.

"Dad's holding something," Colin said.

Amelia set her suspicion aside for the moment and turned her attention to her father, who had lined up some of the dashed steps and was holding a piece of driftwood overhead.

"Is that what I think it is?" asked Bonnie.

"I think it's what you think it is," Clyde said. He looked up at her and she blushed.

Mr. MacGuffin waved the object. It was a stick. Long and straight. It looked like the missing staff. His lips moved, but they were too far away to hear what he was saying.

"The staff!" Bridget said. "Dad found the staff!"

"That's it?" Dash said.

"I sort of expected it to have, like, a big gem on the end," Dot said.

"That's it," Clyde and Mr. King said at once, as if they were twins, but they definitely were not.

When Mr. MacGuffin reached the top of the bluff with the stick, a cheer went up. Amelia looked at Dr. Agatha, to see if she looked as astonished, relieved, and happy as everyone else. Dr. Agatha did not. Was she incapable of these emotions? Did she hate tourists more than she loved Urchin Beach? Or did Dr. Agatha have the real staff and *know* this one was a fake?

With a certainty that made her bones feel heavy, Amelia realized something terrible: The staff was a fake. Her dad had found a stick on the beach. A very nice stick, but not the stick they were looking for, the stick the town needed, the stick that was so important people called it a staff. Mr. MacGuffin was holding what someone in a mystery might call a forgery. An impostor. A fraud.

Was he doing it on purpose? This, Amelia did not know. It was possible, she knew. But it was also possible that he believed he *had* found the town staff.

She looked at the delighted faces of her siblings. She looked at Dot and Dash, who appeared delighted at the delight of everyone else. She looked at Kat, Hayden, and Eugenides, who were exchanging exuberant high fives. She looked at Birdie, who was focusing her lens on Mr. MacGuffin and snapping photos. She looked at all the grown-ups, who were clapping one another on the back and smiling and saying very nice things about Mr. MacGuffin and his extremely well-stocked store.

She looked at Doc. His ears were up. His tongue was out. Even Doc appeared to be thrilled by the stick. Then again, what dog wouldn't want a stick like that?

Amelia exhaled. She would say nothing. She did not wish to be the person who revealed the stick was not, in fact, the one they were all looking for.

Mr. MacGuffin handed the stick to Officer Shirley Locke. "Crime solved," he said. "Mother Nature did it."

Everybody laughed. A few adults peeled away, no doubt heading back to their shops and offices and houses. Mr. MacGuffin took the twins home because it was almost nap time.

Before Amelia could decide what to do, Birdie's mother appeared. She'd been running, so she was breathing hard and had to put her hands on her knees for a moment as she got her wind back.

Then she stood. Her hair, usually in tidy box braids, looked fuzzy and sweaty, and the ankles of her jeans were muddy.

"The slough," Paula Wheeler said. "It's flooded. I checked, and it appears that all the dragonfly nymphs have been washed away."

17

A Total Washout

Bridget was the kind of kid who could fly over the handlebars on her bike and slice open her chin and need stitches—and she wouldn't shed a single tear. She could watch a scary movie and say afterward that her favorite part was when the black cat jumped out from behind the dresser. She didn't even always laugh at funny things. She'd say, "That's funny," and then do a back walkover.

But when Bridget heard about the disaster that had befallen the dragonfly nymphs, she fell down sobbing. Thankfully, nobody told her to keep a stiff upper lip. Amelia glared at Dr. Agatha in case she was thinking about it. Amelia would have taken a swing at Dr. Agatha with the stick Mr. MacGuffin had found if the mystery writer had said anything of the sort.

But Dr. Agatha didn't. In fact, she looked almost as sad as everyone else.

Birdie's mom turned toward town. "I have to file my story," she said. "If anyone has questions or wants to make comments, follow me."

The adults left the kids standing at the edge of the bluff.

"N-n-not the nymphhhhhhhs," Bridget wailed. Doc sat next to her and leaned against her shoulder.

Colin turned toward Dot and Dash. "Bridget's class did a restoration project in the slough. She worked really hard on it."

"What's a slough?" Dash asked.

Bridget tried to answer, but nothing came out except a sob.

"It's marshy land between the forest and the beach," Birdie said. "It's sort of a buffer between dry land and the ocean."

"Estuar-r-r-ry," Bridget wailed.

"What she means," Colin said, "is that it's part of a system called an estuary. Freshwater from creeks and runoff mixes with salty seawater."

"Hab-b-b-b-bitat," Bridget said.

Amelia put a comforting hand on her sister's head. "They're an important habitat," she said. "Everything from eagles and herons to salmon, otters, and oysters live there."

"And the green darner dragonfly." Bridget had stopped sobbing and reached for Amelia's hand.

Amelia pulled her up. "Let's go see for ourselves. Maybe it's not as bad as Mrs. Wheeler says."

Birdie sidled up next to Amelia. "I hope it's not. But my mom's not usually wrong."

Bridget said, "That's not helping, Birdie."

Birdie shrugged. "Don't shoot the messenger."

"Oooooh," Eugenides Turner said.

"How do we get down there?" Dash asked.

Bridget dragged her sleeve across her face and wiped away the snot and tears. "Follow me," she said.

Mr. MacGuffin had used a rope to climb the cliff. He'd left it behind, tied to a post, no doubt because it made it easier to get down to the sand. Sometimes older kids carved handholds in the sandstone, but it wasn't safe. The bluff could be crumbly, especially after a hard rain.

"Who wants to go first?" Amelia asked. She did not.

"Me, duh," Bridget said.

"I'm the oldest," Dash said.

"Technically, Dash, I am five minutes older," Dot said. "I hope you're not playing the male-supremacy card."

"Oops," Dash said. "The patriarchy gets everywhere. It's like glitter. You go first."

"Bridget is going first," Dot said.

"I'm staying here," Colin said. "Someone has to watch Doc."

"Do you want me to stay with you?" Amelia asked.

"I'll stay with him," Kat Bacon said. "I love dogs. And I can tell this one likes me. I felt a distinct zing. Also? I don't want to die."

"Nobody's going to die," Bridget said. "Just hold on to the rope and push off the bluff with your feet. Watch."

One by one, the children lowered themselves down. Little clots of compacted sand sometimes tumbled off the wall, but everyone made it to the beach safely by doing just what Bridget told them to do. When Amelia's turn came, she had to remind herself not to look down. That was the scary part, knowing she was at least thirty feet above the beach. The rope felt rough but sturdy as she went, letting out the slack as she pushed her feet away from the bluff.

"You're doing it!" Dash called.

"Woo!" Dot yelled.

An ocean breeze whipped Amelia's dark hair around her face.

"Breathe," she told herself. "Breathe."

And then her feet touched the sand, and she let go of the rope. She did her best to smooth her hair, but without a mirror, there was no way of knowing whether the part was okay. She pushed her glasses up on her nose and tried not to think about it.

"Let's go already," Bridget said. "And stop biting your fingernail, Amelia. Sheesh."

The kids headed south on the beach, taking care not to step on the clumps of seagrass that lined the edge of the bluff. When they reached the gap in the seagrass, they turned east toward the slough. They hadn't traveled far when the storm damage became apparent.

"Whoa," Eugenides said. "That's a lot of water."

Bridget started running, her sneakers splashing through tea-colored water that was usually damp sand. When Amelia and the rest caught up to her, she was at what had been the edge of the slough, peering into the water.

"I can't see any of the nymphs." Bridget dropped to her knees.

"You're going to be soaked," Amelia said.

"I don't care. The nymphs." She was crying again, her teeth chattering.

"What should we do?" Amelia asked Birdie.

"I can't do anything," Birdie said. "I'm a journalist. I can only write about what other people do."

"This area would probably drain again if somebody moved those logs," Eugenides said.

"Beach logs are dangerous," Amelia said.

Bridget glared. "Not when they're this far from the surf."

"We should get back," Amelia said. "Make a plan." She wanted to take a good look at the staff. See if it had the dragonfly on it after all. If it was the right staff, all would be well. If it wasn't—she wouldn't let herself think about that.

"I want to have a funeral first," Bridget said.

"For the nymphs?" Birdie asked, her pen poised over her notebook.

"For all of us," Bridget said. "When the homes of the smallest creatures are destroyed, the homes of the largest follow."

"Did you read that somewhere?" Dash asked.

"I made it up," Bridget said, "out of pure facts."

"Grim," Dot said.

"Not as grim as my eulogy is about to be," Bridget said. She cleared her throat and clasped her hands over her heart. "It's not fair that the rain flooded your nursery, especially after we did all that work cleaning trash out of it. Dead baby nymphs, I know that human beings are rotten sometimes. They drop their trash and put roads everywhere, and runoff pollutes your little cribs—" This made her sob, and Amelia had to put an arm around Bridget's shoulder so she could continue. "And it seems unfair when Mother Nature dumps too much water on you, and you drown before you ever even get the wings you were meant to fly by." She heaved again, and her shoulders shook.

"But, little nymphs, if any of you can hear me, know that I am thinking good thoughts for you. I am hoping you're still there somewhere. I'm hoping you come back, but I doubt it. And without you, we're in so much trouble. May you rest in peace."

"Wow, Bridget," Dot said. "That was good. Grim. But heartfelt."

Afterward, as they made their way home, Bridget's words rang in Amelia's head like a low bell, tolling doom for Urchin Beach.

Dragonfly Day in True Peril Because of Storm

by Paula Wheeler, Editor in Chief

with additional reporting by Birdie Wheeler

The unseasonably powerful rainstorm on Saturday flooded the slough where Urchin Beach's green darner dragonfly population breeds, killing hundreds of nymphs before they could molt.

"This is a real problem," Mayor Miranda Hoffman said. "They're remarkable creatures. Their bodies have lime-green markings and can grow up to four inches long, with beautiful, lacy wings. Not only are they vital predators in aquatic habitats, but they are also the star attraction of the Dragonfly Day Festival. They're truly a wonder. I just wish I knew what could be done."

The annual festival attracts thousands of attendees from the West Coast, generating most of the town's funding for the library, schools, parks, and services provided by Officer Shirley Locke.

"The theft of the staff started it all. It should have been under lock and key," local Realtor Mike Jung said. "The mayor should lose her job for this."

"Mr. Jung should run against me," Mayor Hoffman said. "I'm not

112

going to step down because it rained. Ugh. Some men. Besides, Dave MacGuffin found the staff on the beach where it had been blown by the storm. Next thing you know, Mr. Jung is going to chant 'lock her up' to Mother Nature."

Last night, in an informal ceremony outside her van, Officer Locke presented Mr. MacGuffin with a good-citizen badge for his efforts in finding the missing dragonfly staff.

"Aw, shucks," Mr. MacGuffin said. "Here's a bucket of gratitude. Get it? It's a literal bucket, Shirl."

"It ruins jokes when you explain them, Dad," Bridget MacGuffin said. "But also? I'm so upset about the dragonflies that I'm not in the mood for your comedy stylings."

After the staff was returned to Glenda's well-built arms, Mayor Hoffman asked, "Who thinks Urchin Beach is going to be lucky again?"

Amelia MacGuffin was overheard saying, "No comment." She declined to elaborate on what she meant.

18

The Thief Strikes Again

The festival was five days away. Inside the MacGuffin family room, Bridget pressed her father about the dragonflies.

"Someone needs to do something about the nymphs," she said.

"Bridget," Mr. MacGuffin said, "there's a lot going on. We can't magically bring them back. We have to focus first on the staircase, and who knows—maybe the slough will drain and everything will be fine. Living creatures are tough little buggers." He laughed. "Get it? Buggers. Because dragonflies are bugs. That's what makes it funny."

Bridget scowled. "You're bugging me an unusual amount right now."

Mr. MacGuffin tousled her hair. "Who wants cocoa?"

Bridget's hand shot up. Everyone else shouted, "YES!"

"I'll make some," Amelia said.

Bridget did a backflip of appreciation. "That's for the cocoa," she said. "And this is for you, Dad." She looked at Mr. MacGuffin and did a terrible somersault that ended with her in the fetal position on the floor. "I call this move the dead dragonfly."

Mr. MacGuffin ignored Bridget. "After cocoa, it's nap time for the twins. So, give them small portions, help them brush their teeth, and tuck them into bed with their blanket scraps, all right?"

"They're not scraps, Dad," Bridget said from her fetal ball. "They're carefully divided halves."

"When you say scraps, it makes them sound like leftovers," Colin added. "The blanket halves aren't left over."

Colin tended to take things literally, but here he was absolutely correct.

Amelia got out the ingredients for cocoa: whole milk, a jug of cream, powdered sugar, and a half pound of dark chocolate buttons.

There were easier ways to make cocoa. You could rip open those little packets. You could heat chocolate syrup in milk. But these were not more delicious ways to make cocoa. If you didn't make cocoa the best way, you'd have regrets.

Amelia did not like regrets.

She poured the milk, cream, and sugar into a pan and clicked on the flame. She stirred and tried to stave off the regretful feeling that was nonetheless knocking a pattern on the door of her heart. SOS, the distress call the Morse twins had thought they'd heard. She stirred more vigorously, keeping a close eye on the mixture. This is the thing with milk—it mustn't boil.

She knew the source of this distress: her secret knowledge that the town staff her father had found was not the right one. She'd examined it closely and was certain. The stain in the wood looked more like a moth than a dragonfly, and she was the only one who seemed to realize it. Worse, time was swiftly running out.

After the twins were down for a nap, she'd *have* to figure out what to do about the fake. Her mind stomped in angry circles while she watched the milk heat. For one thing, she didn't have any suspects. For another, Birdie had been a real pain when she was interviewing people. Amelia understood that it was Birdie's true calling in life to be a journalist, so she put up with it. But that didn't make it fun. She did *not* want to be quoted.

It was too bad Delphine was away. Delphine would have loved to be interviewed, Birdie would have been satisfied, and their friendship would once again be on solid footing. Instead, it felt as if Amelia were descending a sandy bluff with nothing more than a rope and the good sense not to look down. Just one more thing that had gone awry since the theft of the dragonfly staff.

The milk steamed and trembled, and Amelia added the chocolate buttons. She turned off the burner and stirred. The milk turned deeper brown as the chocolate melted. She inhaled.

"That smells fantastic." Bridget crowded her by the stove, but Amelia didn't mind. "How much longer?"

How much longer, indeed. That question could apply to many things, almost none of them pleasant.

"Would you please get the mugs?" Amelia asked. "The special ones we use for soup."

"I'll help," Colin said.

Amelia loved the MacGuffin family mugs. They'd had them longer than she'd been alive. Anything that had lasted that long must be lucky.

The cupboard door was opened. Then there was a crash, the awful sound of things made of heavy clay shattering on the floor. Doc said *Yipe* and shot from the room.

Duncan and Emma, strapped into their high chairs, wailed.

"The mugs!" Colin looked as if he was going to cry.

"It's not my fault," Bridget said. "I opened the cupboard and the shelf collapsed. I didn't mean to do this. I wasn't being reckless. I even used my hands like a regular person, instead of my feet like an acrobat."

"What was that commotion?" Mr. MacGuffin walked into the room, his hair wet from the shower but neatly brushed. And then, "Oh" as he saw the pottery shards on the kitchen floor.

More bad luck. Terrible luck. These were family heirlooms.

"Well," Mr. MacGuffin said, "we have paper cups left from a picnic. We can use those."

"Lucky for us," Bridget said.

Was it, though? Amelia wondered.

After everyone finished their cocoa, and after she and Bridget helped the twins brush their teeth, and after Colin read them their favorite book about socks being pockets for your toes, the twins would not take a nap.

They wanted one. They needed one.

But they would not, could not take one.

Their blanket halves were missing, and even though everyone looked high and low, they were nowhere to be found.

"We'll have Mom bring a new one home from the store," Mr. MacGuffin said. "Blankets are one of our many useful items in stock. Oh, and roofing tar. And replacement shingles." He sighed. "There's a lot of work to do."

Amelia sighed too. The bad luck of the broken mugs and missing blanket and leaking roof proved what she'd feared. Bad luck had made Urchin Beach its home.

If Amelia didn't solve the crime and set things to rights, what would happen next? Maybe even something worse than the death of the dragonfly nymphs. Her sorrows blew in like an ocean storm. They made her shiver all over.

19

The Investigation Wall

That night, Amelia lay awake in bed, thinking and listening to Bridget snore. Amelia could not solve the problem of the dead dragonflies. There was no way to make them live again. But with the right team, they could get the dragonfly staff back. And that was something. It was enough comfort for her to drift off.

The next morning, she felt determined.

"MacGuffin kids," she announced after breakfast, "meet me in the turret in five minutes."

She went outside, flexed her fingers, and took a deep breath. Amelia couldn't believe she was crossing the street. She couldn't believe her freshly flexed hand was curling into a fist. But desperate times called for desperate measures, or so the quote went.

She stood in front of Dot and Dash Morse's house and knocked the SOS code. The door flew open.

"Amelia," Dash said, "are you in distress?"

She nodded.

"What is it?" Dot touched Amelia's forearm in a comforting way.

Amelia found her voice. "The town is in peril," she said, "and the two of you have demonstrated a solid understanding of the process of solving crimes."

"We've read about it," Dash said. "Our old library had a book called *How to Think Like a Master Detective*, by Edith Phipps, PhD."

"Her other book, about cat teleportation, was also excellent," Dot said.

Amelia brightened. "I have that book! The detective one, that is. I got it at the library. And I want us to use it to solve the crime of the stolen dragonfly staff."

"The one your dad found?" Dash said. "I'm confused."

Amelia took a deep breath. "I don't think that's the right staff."

"Whoa," Dash said. "That's gotta be awkward."

It *was* awkward. Dash understood her so well. "My dad wasn't trying to trick anyone. He got excited. Dads sometimes do."

"So do moms," Dot said.

Dash nodded. "And how."

"Can you come over?" Amelia asked. "Help us solve the case?"

"We'd love to," Dot and Dash said simultaneously.

Amelia wanted to jump up and down from excitement. But you don't do that in front of seventh graders unless they do it first.

"We'll make an investigation wall," Dash said.

"Okay," Amelia said. "But I don't know what that is."

"We'll tell you on the way," Dot said. "Dash, get the sticky notes and Sharpies."

"On it," he said.

A few minutes later, they'd gathered in the MacGuffins' turret. Buckets still stood about the room, in case of more rain. The children sat on cushions arranged in a semicircle, and Colin handed out graham crackers from a package he'd fetched as soon as he saw there were guests. Doc walked from person to person, asking for a bite of graham cracker.

"That took longer than five minutes," Bridget said. "It was more like seven."

Sometimes Bridget was kind of a pain. Amelia pressed her lips together, not wanting to get in an argument in front of the Morse twins.

"But we were worth the wait, weren't we?" Dash scratched Doc behind the ears, and Doc responded by melting across Dash's lap like a piece of warm cheese.

"Well, yeah, I guess," Bridget said.

"Good, then," Dot said.

"Good, then," Emma said. Duncan clapped.

"I still don't know why we're here." Bridget crossed her arms. "Amelia didn't say."

"We're going to make an investigation wall," Dash said. Then he made his voice get silly as he rubbed Doc's belly. "Aren't we, Doc?"

Amelia cleared her throat. "Colin. Can you give the twins something to play with? This is serious work."

"Absolutely. I'll get the block dispenser." It was one of his inventions. The twins loved it, and Amelia was glad Colin got a chance to show it off in front of their neighbors. He set it up for Duncan and Emma, and they got it working.

Then Amelia held up *How to Think Like a Master Detective*. "I know that some of you are familiar with this book. Some of you are not." She looked at Bridget. "But this is what we're going to use to solve the Case of the Missing Dragonfly Staff."

That was what she would have called the mystery if she were the detective on a television show or in a book. It felt strange and delicious to describe it that way out loud. As if it were a real mystery in the world and not just a lonely wish in her heart.

Amelia continued. "We have four days left. It's not a lot of time, but—"

"Earth to Amelia," Bridget interrupted. "Dad already found it."

"Amelia thinks the stick he found is not the right one," Dash said.

"That makes one of us," Bridget said. "Dad isn't dumb, and he would never lie. Besides, the real problem is the dragonfly nymphs, not the dragonfly staff."

"Hold up, Bridget," Amelia said. "Let me read this bit to you."

She opened the detective book to page 147: "'Many times in the course of my experience studying criminal investigations, I have watched people jump to conclusions. In detecting, one should not jump. One should step carefully from clue to clue, as one crosses a river using available boulders. Just as jumping on a wet boulder can cause one to slip and be carried away by rushing water, jumping to conclusions can cause a miscarriage of justice. It is understandable. One *wants* to solve a crime. One *leaps* for the first answer. We must *resist* this temptation.'"

Amelia tapped the page. "I think what happened here is that Dad *wanted* the stick he found to be the dragonfly staff. So did everyone else," she said. "So, he leapt to a conclusion. Meanwhile, a thief is walking free."

Doc yawned.

"My sentiments exactly, Doc," Bridget said. "I'm out." She took herself to a corner and practiced a handstand.

Amelia felt a flash of something complicated: anger, frustration, and doubt. What if Bridget was right?

"I have sticky notes," Dot said. "Let's put them on the wall in four columns. Suspect, Motive, Opportunity, Evidence. For each suspect, we'll list their motive to take the staff, the opportunity they had to do it, and the evidence we've gathered."

"Cool," Colin said.

Amelia nodded, relieved no one else had abandoned ship.

"Who has a suspect?" Dash asked. Then he grimaced and waved his hand in front of his face. "Oh. I think Doc might have gas."

"Sorry," Amelia said.

"What about that Realtor guy, Mr. Jung?" Dot asked. "He hates the mayor, judging by what I read in the *Gazette*."

"About that," Amelia said. "He and the mayor are actually a couple. Birdie told me once. They like to trash-talk each other for fun, and Birdie's mom allows it in the paper because it makes for better copy."

"In addition," Colin said, "Mr. Jung wouldn't do anything to keep tourists away. That would hurt his business. Sometimes they love it so much here they decide to move to Urchin Beach. That's how he makes a living."

"True story," Dash said. "That's why our moms moved us here from Seattle. They wanted to get away from the hustle and bustle."

"And look at us now," Dot said. "Investigating crime and dealing with natural disasters. This is awesome."

"We're hustlin'," Dash said.

"And bustlin'," Dot said. "But, okay, who was that crabby old lady at the beach yesterday? She looked suspicious."

"Dr. Agatha." Amelia pointed at the manor. "She's our other neighbor."

Dot wrote *Dr. Agatha* on a sticky note and pressed it to the wall. "What's her motive?"

"She writes books about murderers?" Colin said.

"Writing books isn't a *crime*," Bridget said, "even if some of the books they make us read at school should be *outlawed* for being *criminally boring*." She was still in a handstand, and her voice sounded strained.

"Dr. Agatha strongly dislikes tourists," Amelia said.

"That's good," Dash said. "That's a motive. The dragonfly staff is mostly a tourist thing, right?"

Amelia nodded.

Dot tapped her cheek thoughtfully. "What about opportunity? Did anyone witness her near the staff?"

"Oh!" Amelia said. She'd recalled that during the storm, a single light was on in Dr. Agatha's whole house. "She might have done it on Saturday morning during the storm. The light was on in her office, but I didn't see her in it."

Dot wrote down *Saturday morning* and asked, "Does anyone have evidence supporting this theory?"

"A gray hair, plucked from the scene of the crime, perhaps?" Dash suggested.

Amelia knew he was teasing her, and she laughed. Not all teasing was bad teasing.

"Dr. Agatha is a crime expert," Colin said. "If there are any clues, they're probably in her house because she knows we can't get them there."

"Oh, can't we?" Dash said.

Amelia gulped. She had a hunch about what was coming. So, apparently, did Bridget.

Bridget came out of her handstand with a thump. "This is a crummy idea, everyone."

"That's okay," Dash said. "No one should do anything they don't consent to doing. So, here's the plan."

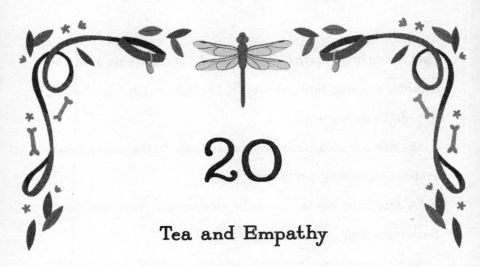

20

Tea and Empathy

Amelia had never knocked on Dr. Agatha's door without at least an offering. A loaf of bread. Molasses cookies. A bouquet of tulips on May Day.

This time, her hands were empty, although she had tucked *How to Think Like a Master Detective* beneath one arm. She thought it would send a message that she knew about crime and therefore would be difficult to murder.

Amelia also had backup in the form of Dot and Dash, who were hiding in the shrubbery. Colin had stayed behind with the twins and the block dispenser, and Bridget—well, she was wherever she'd stomped off to. It would have been nice to have Bridget by her side, as she'd been when they'd first met Dot and Dash. Bridget could be so stubborn.

The plan was for Amelia to get inside and distract the author.

Amelia would take care to leave the door open a titch. Then, when it was safe, Dot and Dash would slip in and hunt for clues or even the dragonfly staff itself.

When they'd made the plan, Amelia had felt hope for the first time in days, even with Bridget being a stick in the mud. Now, though, Amelia felt queasy. She knew she'd have to knock. By herself. She didn't want to. She looked at her fist, hoping it would coax itself into action. As she stood there, holding her breath, the door swung open.

"Were you ever going to knock? Or were you going to stare at your knuckles all day?"

Dr. Agatha might have been short, but her presence was substantial. Inside, her house was shadowy, but sunlight glazed the doorway, making her look scarier than ever in her cardigan and joggers. She also wore a pointy white blouse, finished with a necktie that had been pierced with a glittering golden pin in the shape of a key. On her feet were slippers, fat and furry ones. Amelia suspected Dr. Agatha had murdered a stuffie and was wearing its feet as a trophy.

"I suppose I should invite you in," Dr. Agatha said. "Shoes off, please. There are slippers in the basket."

There were more, and they looked exactly like Dr. Agatha's.

Amelia grimaced as she slipped into a pair, imagining the scream of the stuffed bear at the moment of its untimely death.

"Are you going to stand there like an indolent mime," Dr. Agatha said, "or are you going to tell me the reason for your visit? My powers of observation have already informed me that you are not bearing carbohydrates or flora. Therefore, you are in need."

"I—" Amelia said.

So many words could have followed: *must get going* or *wanted to know what time it was* or *think I've made a huge mistake.*

Amelia considered the consequence of each. Then she decided, with resignation, that the truth was the best path. It was what the detective book called inevitable: *The truth remains when all that is untrue has been wiped away. This is what a good detective does: scrubs off the filth of mystery and the scum of crime to leave a sparkling rightness in its wake.*

"I—"

"You said that already." Dr. Agatha glanced at the book under Amelia's arm. She made a sound. A sort of scoffing, sniffing sound. "If you wanted to learn how to solve a crime, you didn't need *that.* You could have asked me."

"Oh, this old thing?" Amelia said. "I forgot I had it."

"I suppose you'll be wanting cookies," Dr. Agatha said. "And it's foolish to eat cookies without a cup of tea. And no one should drink tea unless it's been thoroughly laced with sugar and cream. That is practically criminal."

Well, she would know about criminal, Amelia thought.

Dr. Agatha studied her with her hard green eyes. "Follow me, then."

Amelia looked back at the door. She pretended to close it all the way.

"Coming," she said.

Amelia hugged the book as she followed Dr. Agatha from the entryway to the kitchen. Dr. Agatha's house was gloomy, crisscrossed with wooden beams the color of chocolate. Intricate rugs covered the floors with hues of red and blue and purple and turquoise. Bookshelves lined almost every wall, and the rest were full of painted portraits of people who looked as though they had been dead for ages.

Were their eyes following Amelia as she moved? Almost certainly. The taxidermied animals scattered about also unsettled her: a bear standing in the corner with its arms up high, a snowy owl coming in for a landing, and a possum with an appalling smile. Amelia started. Was he wearing glossy wing-tip shoes? Yes, he was.

"You squeaked," Dr. Agatha said.

"Did I?" Amelia asked.

"Like a mouse." Dr. Agatha pushed a swinging door with a round window in it. "After you."

They were in the kitchen. Despite her fear, Amelia sighed. The kitchen was in no way creepy. It was lovely.

"Nice, isn't it?" Dr. Agatha said. "It's my favorite place."

The wall over the sink was made of windows that framed Dr. Agatha's backyard. Amelia had seen this window from the turret. But she'd never been able to look inside. Now she could see the turret window, but the angle was such that she could not see past it. When she and Dr. Agatha were in their favorite places, they could be aware of each other without seeing each other, she realized. It felt significant, although she did not know why, as though it were a clue to an entirely different mystery.

A long table with a sturdy wooden top ran down the center of the room, holding bowls of fruit and canisters with wooden spoons and spatulas and things that looked useful. Shelves along each wall displayed pots, pans, teapots, teacups, and cake stands and plates made of painted china.

"My dad would like it here." She was certain.

"But do *you* like it?" Dr. Agatha asked. The shadow of a smile flickered on her face.

Amelia hesitated. She had the feeling that Dr. Agatha *wanted* her to like it. If Dr. Agatha wanted her to like the kitchen, her favorite place, then perhaps it meant that Dr. Agatha wanted Amelia to like *her* too. That made Amelia feel even worse about her scheme with Dot and Dash.

It was true that Dr. Agatha had once said that MacGuffins were insignificant. That was mean. But searching someone's house for evidence of a crime was in a whole different league. Amelia managed to nod.

"Would you like that cup of tea now?" Dr. Agatha asked.

Amelia nodded again. Then the ceiling creaked, as though someone above was creeping about. Amelia froze. Dr. Agatha lit a flame under the kettle. She did not seem to have noticed.

Amelia swallowed hard. In the daylight that streamed in, Dr. Agatha's eyes looked almost friendly. Maybe Dr. Agatha was mean on a part-time basis, the way Miss Fortune opened the library only on Mondays, Wednesdays, Fridays, and Sundays.

"Arrange the cookies on a plate, then," Dr. Agatha said. Amelia was used to bossiness from Bridget.

"While we're waiting for the water to heat," Dr. Agatha said, "I'll tell you about that book underneath your arm. I know the author."

Amelia still couldn't manage anything more than a nod. It wasn't surprising that Dr. Agatha knew the author. She supposed there was probably an author society they all belonged to.

But the next thing Dr. Agatha said, as she put pretty cups on plates, did surprise Amelia.

"She's my sister."

21

A Tale of Two Sisters

Dr. Agatha told Amelia the story as she put tea leaves into the pot
to steep. Dr. Agatha and Edith had grown up as close as fingers and
thumbs, and just as frequently opposed to each other. Dr. Agatha
was the elder one. Edith was second but always wanted to keep up
with Agatha. The Urchin Beach manor was where they'd spent their
summers.

Their father had been the finest detective ever to work in Seattle.
He solved murders. Bank robberies. Cases involving forged art and
stolen elephants. He tracked down kidnapped children by solving
clues left by wicked abductors.

"He was always working." Dr. Agatha placed clever strainers over
their cups and poured tea. "Cream?"

Amelia nodded; she could tell Dr. Agatha had more to say.

"My sister and I lost our mother when we were very small, and I suppose we were always in competition for our father's attention. We both became experts in *being* detectives, although neither of us *became* a detective. That takes far more nerve than I ever possessed."

Amelia hadn't expected to hear that. Dr. Agatha seemed like she had a lot of nerve. She wrote books. She intimidated the whole town, especially on sidewalks.

"My sister became interested in other things." Dr. Agatha made a face. "Cats, mostly. And while I am also an aficionado of cats and have one of my own, Edith went down a path regarding an obscure feline science that was not wide enough for the both of us. We haven't spoken a word to each other in years."

Amelia couldn't imagine life without any of her siblings. The paths at Urchin Beach were wide enough for all of them. Maybe not if they were holding hands, but even if they had to walk single file, they always went in the same direction.

Well, almost always. Bridget hadn't wanted to help solve the dragonfly staff mystery. She said she had more important things to do, and even though Dash was right about consent, Amelia had hurt feelings. Was this the start of a fork in the path for her and Bridget? The thought made her mouth too dry even to swallow. She reached for her tea.

"When our father passed away," Dr. Agatha said, "we had nothing to compete for, and instead of finding something new to bind us, we drifted apart." She sipped her tea. "But that isn't why you're here. Clearly you're solving a mystery, and I think I know which one."

Thump!

Dr. Agatha and Amelia both looked up. Then they looked at each other.

"That was probably my cat, Crumpet," Dr. Agatha said. "He's not usually so clumsy, though. The noise worries me." She stood. "Excuse me."

"Wait!" Amelia's voice shook.

"It'll be a moment," Dr. Agatha said. "I want to make sure he isn't stuck somewhere."

"The thing is—" Amelia rummaged for an excuse. "I love cats. I really, really do. Can I go with you?"

Dr. Agatha cocked her head and looked at Amelia. "I suppose. But don't touch anything in my library. I'm in the middle of a chapter and need everything to stay as it is."

"No problem," Amelia said, frantic to keep Dr. Agatha from catching the Morses.

As they walked upstairs, Amelia used her heaviest, loudest feet to warn the others, but it was useless. The slippers muffled the noise. "Here, kitty, kitty," she called out. "HERE, KITTY, KITTY."

"Maybe not so loud," Dr. Agatha said. "Cats have dignity. They're not like dogs."

They paused outside Dr. Agatha's library, a room with double doors that were open. Bookshelves ran around the room from floor to ceiling, except for the wall that held a wide window overlooking the town and, beyond that, the ocean. There was also a fancy exercise bicycle and some free weights. Apparently this was also where Dr. Agatha worked out.

Amelia stared out the window. "You can see Glenda from here." Amelia could also make out the countdown to Dragonfly Day sign. Four days. She gulped.

Dr. Agatha stood by Amelia. "Yes, I can see that hideous wooden primate."

"Did you see the person who stole the dragonfly staff?" Amelia asked.

"I did not see any such person," she said.

Then Amelia noticed two sets of sneakers poking out from beneath the drapes. Her stomach folded itself into an origami starfish. If either of them moved or sneezed or even breathed hard, they'd be caught.

Amelia grabbed Dr. Agatha by her sleeve. "I think I heard your cat!"

She pulled Dr. Agatha along, and to Amelia's great relief, a sphinx-like, hairless cat with deadly ice-blue eyes sat staring at them from the end of the hall. He lifted one paw and licked it slowly.

"There you are, Crumpet," Dr. Agatha said.

"May I hold him?" Amelia asked.

"You can try," Dr. Agatha said. "But he is a particular beast. He doesn't trust just anyone."

Amelia approached him slowly. She crouched and held out her arms. She made a kissing sound, the sort that always worked with Doc. Crumpet shot off through an open door. Amelia was mortified.

"Ha!" Dr. Agatha said. "No sale. I say we get back to our tea."

"All right." Amelia stole a glance at the library as they passed it. The shoes hadn't moved. The stress was going to melt her skull. She couldn't help but notice that Dr. Agatha also peeked at the curtains. If she'd noticed the shoes, though, she said nothing.

Back in the kitchen, Dr. Agatha poured more tea.

"You may add the cream yourself," Dr. Agatha said. "I like a lot."

"Me too," Amelia said. She blew on her cup and took a sip.

"What do you think of the staff your father found yesterday?" Dr. Agatha asked.

From the way Dr. Agatha looked at her, Amelia could tell it was another test. "I thought it looked . . . nice," she said.

"Pah!" Dr. Agatha said. "Nice. A word that once meant 'ignorant.' You don't strike me as being an ignorant person, Amelia MacGuffin. You know as well as I do that the staff is not the right one."

"I don't think my dad would intentionally mislead people," she said.

"I should say not. He's salt of the earth. As upstanding as they come. And he makes an excellent Ligurian focaccia. Which is why I did not use the words *fake* or *fraud*. I don't believe it was an intentional deception. But the stick he found is not our missing staff. Do you agree with me or not on this matter?"

"Well . . ." Amelia struggled to answer. She didn't want to criticize her dad in front of Dr. Agatha. But she also didn't want to lie.

"People generally see what they want to see," Dr. Agatha said. "And that is what separates a world-class detective from the average person . . . the ability to see what is there and what is not, and why both matter."

Amelia glanced at the cookies, and Dr. Agatha slid the plate toward her. "I think your father found a stick that looked like the missing staff, and people were all too willing to accept it because it's an easy solution to a difficult problem."

"That is maybe true." Amelia took a cookie. If this was what it felt like to be interrogated, she was going to need sustenance.

"The question is," Dr. Agatha said, "does it matter if the staff is the right one or merely one that's good enough?"

Amelia chewed her cookie and thought. Then she answered, as truthfully as she could. "Not if people believe it, I guess. I mean, it does seem unlikely that there is really magic behind the staff."

"We are in agreement," Dr. Agatha said. "But that doesn't change the fact that there's a thief about, does it?"

Amelia nodded—not because she was afraid to speak this time, but because her mouth was full.

"And that is a problem, is it not?"

Amelia followed Dr. Agatha's line of thought. The presence of a thief meant more things would be stolen. It also meant someone in their midst had gotten away with an injustice. Amelia couldn't stand the thought of that.

"I thought I'd found out who did it, but I was wrong," Amelia said.

She told Dr. Agatha about examining the scene of the crime. About the red hair she'd found. How she thought it was a clue that led her to the Morse twins.

"A red hairing," Dr. Agatha said. "Very common."

Amelia knew that red hair was not all that common, but she and Dr. Agatha were getting on so well that she decided to let it go.

"Who are your other suspects?" Dr. Agatha looked at her intently.

Amelia's cheeks blazed. "Well," she said.

Dr. Agatha laughed. "Me?" she said. "I suppose I should be honored. Someone of my age and renown, a criminal! No doubt that's what those children who'd been hiding in the shrubbery were doing in my library just now—looking for evidence?"

Amelia felt herself turn purple from her hairline to her toes.

"It's quite all right," Dr. Agatha said. "You wouldn't believe how many places I've sneaked into in my day. But I didn't steal the staff. I detest the flocks of tourists that descend upon us, but I'd rather scare them off the old-fashioned way—with my unpleasant demeanor."

Amelia took in this information. Dr. Agatha was scary on purpose. That explained a lot, and it also made Amelia think that the mystery writer might turn out to be an ally.

"We couldn't think of any other suspects," she said.

"Sometimes," Dr. Agatha said, "when I am plotting a book, I make a list of possible motives first. Then I match them to potential suspects. It's easier than the other way around."

Amelia looked out the window. "Okay. Someone could hate Urchin Beach."

"Too vague," Dr. Agatha said. "People tend to be very specific when they commit crimes."

"Someone might have thought the stick was pretty."

"Your father found an equally pretty stick on the beach without trying."

"Someone might have wanted to make Officer Locke look bad," Amelia said.

Dr. Agatha chuckled. "I don't know that someone would have had to try very hard to do that." Then her expression turned serious. "I shouldn't have said that out loud. That wasn't kind. It was a good thought you had, however. Personal animosity is a powerful motive for crime."

"Someone might have wanted to make the mayor look bad," Amelia said.

"I like the sound of that," Dr. Agatha said. "The mayor is even more powerful than Officer Locke. Who would dislike the mayor? And don't say that Jung fellow. I've seen him and the mayor canoodling. I know that they're secret sweethearts."

"I can't think of anyone," Amelia said. "Doesn't everyone like Mayor Hoffman? She's an extremely accomplished woman."

Dr. Agatha sighed. "I think you'll find as you get older that many people dislike accomplished women because of what they have achieved. I'm not suggesting that is the case here. But remind me, child, who ran against her in the last election?"

Amelia didn't want to. She looked out the window at the hedge, which was shaking as if there were a strong wind. But the clouds overhead hung still, as though they'd been painted there. The movement on a windless day struck Amelia as strange.

"Oh, that's right," Dr. Agatha said. "It was your mother."

"She wouldn't have taken the staff," Amelia said.

"But," Dr. Agatha said slowly, as if she was choosing her words with care, "that would give your father motive to replace it if he thought she had. People do all sorts of things for love."

Amelia could not deny that was true. But her mother? A thief? She far preferred suspecting the Morse twins. She could think of a thousand reasons her mother hadn't done it. Wouldn't do it. Mrs. MacGuffin had been disappointed when she wasn't elected mayor, but she had cheered up in about five minutes and was one of the first to congratulate Mayor Hoffman.

"A truly good detective doesn't let personal attachments cloud her vision," Dr. Agatha said. "Do you want to catch a thief or not?"

A troubling memory surfaced. The day the staff was stolen, her mother had instructed the family to stay out of the shed. Amelia had forgotten about it. Now she remembered. And she wondered why her mother had said this. It was normal for her mother to say such things around the holidays. The shed was where she stored presents. But the Dragonfly Day Festival wasn't a gift-giving occasion.

Amelia felt sick. She wished she hadn't eaten so many cookies. She wished she hadn't thickened her tea with so much cream. She wished, most of all, that she didn't care so much about everything: solving the crime, saving the town, protecting her family, getting to keep Doc. Caring about everything so much all the time was hard.

Her chin wobbled. "Dr. Agatha, what would happen if I left this mystery unsolved?"

"It's hard to say for certain," Dr. Agatha said. "But generally, people do what they can get away with. So, we can expect more thefts, which will lead to distrust between neighbors. And that is the sort of thing that ruins a community as surely as a lack of funds. There's no magic more fragile than trust."

"Have you ever not been able to solve one of the mysteries in your books?"

Dr. Agatha shook her head. "My mind would never let go. It would keep spinning and spinning until I found the answer. That's how stories work, my dear. They want to find their endings."

"But this isn't a story," Amelia said. "It's real life."

"That's what some people might say." Dr. Agatha drank the last of her tea. "But real life isn't just what happens to us. It's what we tell ourselves about who we are and what we want the world to be.

And those are the questions in front of you now, my dear. The next chapter is yours to write."

It was late in the afternoon. Less light found its way through the window. The hedge was shadow blackened and still.

"Doc!" It was Colin's voice.

"Here, boy!" That was Dash.

"Come and get some cheese!" And that was Dot.

That meant they'd left the house. Amelia supposed it didn't matter because Dr. Agatha knew they'd been sneaking around. Even so, she felt relief.

"Thank you for the cookies, the tea, and the advice," Amelia said. "It's probably time for me to go home."

"It probably is," Dr. Agatha said. "But I have enjoyed our time together, and I hope you come again."

"See," Amelia said. "MacGuffins aren't insignificant, are we?"

Dr. Agatha looked surprised. "Whatever would have made you think that?"

Amelia blushed. "You said it to me once when we passed on the sidewalk."

"Most likely," she said, "I was talking with myself about my work. I do that sometimes. I walk and I talk to myself about plot twists and turns. In a mystery, a MacGuffin is an insignificant object used as a storyteller's device. It's a saying. But in real life? There's no reason a MacGuffin can't be the most significant soul of all."

Most significant felt good to Amelia at first as she walked home, her mind straining under the weight of the mystery and Dr. Agatha's words. But as she got closer to her own front door, she understood that perhaps Dr. Agatha had meant *most significant* in a bad way.

After all, a villain was the most significant person in a story from the perspective of the hero. That was the person who did the deed that must be undone. Who'd committed the crime that must be solved. In this instance, that person might very well be her mother.

Amelia could think of no more likely suspect as she stood on the porch. Behind her were the Morses' house and a breeze from the ocean. Ahead, her own front door. She stared at it and closed her eyes to make a wish.

When she opened them again, she went inside, wondering who she was—and who she would become. Four days. That's all the time she had left to find out.

22

Amelia Homes In

Amelia called a tentative "hello" to everyone.

"I hope you're not as muddy as Bridget," her mother called.

"Nope," Amelia said.

"Sit with us," Colin said. He and the Morse twins were by the fireplace, building structures out of graham crackers. The rest of the family was in the kitchen.

Her mother. Could she be a thief?

"You're alive!" Colin whispered. "We were beginning to worry."

"That was a close call in the study," Dot said.

"She knew you were there," Amelia said.

"Really?" Dot said. "But we were so stealthy."

"Except for that time you dropped a dumbbell," Dash said.

"I wanted to see if I could lift it," Dot said.

"That explains the bump we heard," Amelia said. "Dr. Agatha said she thought it was her cat. But Crumpet didn't strike me as clumsy. He looked like a sleek goblin."

"Are they going to get in trouble?" Colin asked.

"No," Amelia said. "She told me she'd broken into plenty of places."

"I had no idea that people that age had that kind of moxie," Dot said. "That's goals."

"We didn't find any evidence," Dash said. "We didn't find the staff either."

Amelia was not surprised.

Dot slid the *Gazette* across the table. "And the thief is still at large." In it was an article Birdie had written by herself—something that made Amelia feel proud even as it was terribly discouraging.

Rash of Thefts Plagues Urchin Beach

by Birdie Wheeler, News Intern

Urchin Beach officer Shirley Locke is warning residents to lock their doors, windows, and bicycles after a rash of thefts around town.

"We haven't seen anything like this before. Not in our hundred-year history," Locke said. "We're investigating, but in the meantime, people need to be vigilant."

The list of missing and presumed-stolen items includes sporting goods, clothing, yarn, firewood, and food from Clyde's Crab 'N' Go. Mayor Miranda Hoffman's keys are also missing, but Locke said the mayor is known to misplace them from time to time.

"She oughtta wear them around her neck," local Realtor Mike Jung said. "That's what all the best mayors do. Someone ought to give her a lanyard. Someone who cares about her, that is."

Most of the thefts have occurred on the northeast side of town, between town hall, the library, and the Pacific General Store.

Amelia put down the paper. Those were all places her mother frequented.

"The article didn't say anything about the twins' half blankets," Colin said. "At first I thought they'd been misplaced, but now I think they've been stolen. I think you should tell Birdie, like a news tip."

Amelia agreed that theft seemed likely. And she would call Birdie to congratulate her and pass along the tip. But something didn't add up. The twins loved their blanket pieces. Why would Mrs. MacGuffin have stolen the blanket halves? What was her motive? Did Mrs. MacGuffin want to throw suspicion on to someone else? Or was it because she thought the twins were getting too old for them? Was she tired of looking for them at nap time? Each seemed plausible.

Mrs. MacGuffin also had many opportunities. Amelia steeled herself. It meant she needed to search for evidence.

If only she could talk things over with someone. Someone less scary than Dr. Agatha. Birdie had made it clear she didn't want to speculate or become part of the story. Delphine was still at sea and couldn't be reached. And her family—no one would want to believe Mrs. MacGuffin might be the Urchin Beach thief.

No, she was on her own. Her mother *was* a suspect. Everyone else thought the staff had been found and returned. No one would be looking for it. It was up to Amelia to solve the crime and close the case. Alone. Doc ambled over and laid his head in her lap.

Well, not entirely alone, she thought as she scratched him behind the ears. *I have Doc. At least for now.*

That night at dinner, Mr. MacGuffin stretched and yawned. "Tomorrow's gonna be a big day," he said.

"Every day feels like a big day lately," Mrs. MacGuffin said. "What I'd really like is a day off. I want to steal away somewhere. Just slip out like a family of fugitives. I'd do anything for a rest."

Amelia wilted. She looked at her plate of tacos. Usually she loved tacos. But tonight she couldn't eat.

"Well, not until after the festival," Mr. MacGuffin said. "But yes, I'd kill for a day off."

Now both her parents were talking like criminals.

"What's happening tomorrow?" Bridget asked. "I have plans." She shoved half a taco into her mouth.

"First, if it's not raining, I patch the roof. It should be easy unless I fall off." Mr. MacGuffin laughed. "Then I'm leading the crew to rebuild the staircase to the beach. If we get it done in time and if the bluff doesn't collapse, the festival will happen as planned and all will be well."

His jokes about falling off the roof and collapsing bluffs weren't funny. The thought of her dad up on the roof of the turret or building a dangerous staircase made Amelia's limbs feel tingly, like someone had screwed them into the wrong sockets.

"Amelia and I will head to the address on Doc's microchip," Mrs. MacGuffin said.

Amelia raised her eyebrows. That was news to her. So soon?

"That is, if you still want to go," Mrs. MacGuffin said.

"I do," Amelia said.

"Me too," Bridget said. "But I'll be otherwise engaged."

"I want to go," Colin said.

"Go," the twins said. "Go."

"Sorry, kids. I've called Maya already," Mrs. MacGuffin said. "At least some of you need to be here for her. Otherwise, she'll be lonely, and she'll have to eat the brownies Dad is baking all by herself."

"Lucky ducks," Bridget said. "Maya is easy meat. Colin and the twins can go nuts."

Mr. MacGuffin spat out the sip of diet sarsaparilla he'd taken. Then he coughed violently.

"I won't go nuts," Colin said, thumping Mr. MacGuffin's back. "I'll probably make Doc a sign that says, 'Welcome Home for Good This Time.'"

"Do I have permission to leave the house at one p.m.?" Bridget asked. "It's for a good cause."

What good cause? Amelia wondered. Bridget's idea of a good cause was talking Clyde out of free candy bars.

"You'll be making safe choices?" Mrs. MacGuffin asked.

"Duh," Bridget said.

Mrs. MacGuffin looked as though she wanted to say something more, but she didn't. She looked tired. The way someone who'd been running all over town stealing things might. Amelia felt guilty thinking such thoughts, but the detective manual warned readers against letting feelings get in the way. *This is what a detective has*, the book said. *Observations. A keen understanding of human* nature. *The Big Connection, when all the facts come together to form a Picture of Guilt.*

It was an enormous weight on her shoulders. But she had to bear it. So much depended on it, and even if there was no real luck in the staff, she didn't want to take any chances, not when people were climbing on roofs and fixing treacherous staircases and counting on eager tourists at the Dragonfly Day Festival.

That night, as she lay in bed, trying not to be too annoyed by Bridget's snoring, Amelia came up with something of a plan. It would require her to wake early. She wished Bridget would help, but her sister was stubborn.

Amelia couldn't help but think of the rift that had come between Dr. Agatha and Edith Phipps, PhD. There would be time to fix things with Bridget later, she reasoned. For now, there was a thief to stop. At dawn, she'd ask Colin to do his part. Then she'd visit the Morse twins again and enlist them as her allies.

She was going to break into the shed.

23

A Moment with the Thief

The thief had amassed quite the trove of goods. They were hidden away, each one a treasure—especially the dragonfly staff. It was the thief's first trophy from Urchin Beach. It was special. Something about it filled the thief with a feeling they'd come to love: the feeling of being lucky.

The thief could have stopped after the staff. But no.

Instead, the thief collected many objects. Jackets. Vintage buoys. Decorations meant for the Dragonfly Day Festival: strings of lights and even a colorful cloth bunting from a victim's porch.

The thief felt a pang about stealing the MacGuffin twins' blankets. Like everyone in Urchin Beach, the thief loved the MacGuffins. And the youngest were so adorable. But the opportunity had presented itself, and it was that simple.

What was the thief to do when such a thing happened—turn it down? Of course not.

Besides, the twins weren't babies anymore. Did they really need blankets?

What was the thief's motive? you ask.

Even the thief wasn't sure. It might have been the thrill of finding something unguarded. It might have been the joy of possessing precious things. It might have been the feeling of having a purpose in life.

Whatever the reason, the thief stole by day. The thief stole by night. The thief believed in taking opportunities that presented themselves. After all, success lived at the intersection of preparation and opportunity—that plus a healthy dose of luck.

The most astonishing part of all of it: No one suspected the thief.

People smiled as they passed by. Waved. Gave greetings like, "Well, hello, friend."

The thief had never been so happy.

The thief had never felt so lucky.

Urchin Beach is a wonderful place, the thief thought. *The best in the world.*

And then the thief slipped out once more, in search of another treasure to take.

24

To Pick a Lock

Morning arrived, reluctant and gray. Amelia read *How to Think Like a Master Detective* to get her mind into the right zone. She was surprised to learn that the term wasn't *red hairing*; it was *red herring*, and it meant a misleading clue. Either way, the red hair she'd found had been exactly that.

When she heard Colin stirring, she slipped into his room. She opened the book to the relevant page and asked if he'd build the device described.

"I'd love to," he said.

Then, while Bridget tried to convince her parents she needed a shovel, Amelia strode out the front door with Doc on his leash.

"I'm taking him for a walk!" she announced. "Be back soon!"

Doc was her cover. She obviously couldn't say that she intended to break into the shed and see if their mother was a criminal.

"You're a good boy, Doc." She meant it. He *was* a good boy. He didn't bark except for a low *whuff* when he wanted to go outside to relieve himself. He always came back when they called him. He was gentle with Duncan and Emma, and he seemed a great comfort to Colin as well as an attentive companion to Bridget.

He was part of the family already, and one of the reasons for the shivering teacup feeling in her stomach was the fact that they might have to say goodbye to him.

She looked both ways and crossed the street. When she knocked the SOS code on Dot and Dash's door, she put her hand on Doc's furry back for comfort. He had such nice fur. A mix of so many colors.

The door swung open. It was Dash, still in his pajamas. Amelia wanted to die, but there was no time for that.

"Can you do me a favor?" she asked.

Dot arrived at the door, also in pajamas. "What's up, Amelia?"

"She needs a favor," Dash said.

This felt like such an enormous risk to ask. What if they said no?

"Anything you need," Dot said. "Cup of sugar? A couple of eggs?"

"More breaking and entering?" Dash asked.

Amelia shook her head. "Do you know the code for 'someone's coming'?"

"Easy," Dash said. He tapped a pattern on the frame of the door.

That didn't sound easy. It sounded enormously complicated.

Dash laughed and tapped again.

... --- -- . --- -. . .----. ... / -.-. --- -- .. -. --.

"Show-off," Dot said.

"I need to break into the shed in our backyard," Amelia said. "Can one of you keep watch and tap out a warning if someone's coming?"

"Ooh, is the shed off-limits?" Dot asked.

Amelia nodded.

"Is there something dangerous in there?" Dash asked.

"Paint, but I have no plans to use it internally," Amelia said.

"Is this related to the crime spree?" Dot asked.

Amelia didn't want to say. She also didn't want to lie to these kids. They were the nicest seventh graders she'd ever met. "If it is, I'll let you know."

"Well, then we're in," Dash said. "The Morse family code is to follow your curiosity."

"And, when in doubt, to ask for forgiveness instead of permission," Dot said.

That was fascinating. What would it be like to live among Morses? Her own curiosity often felt like a hot stove—something useful, but something she needed to be careful around. With five kids, her parents didn't have a lot of time to deal with the consequences of curiosity.

"Well, great," Amelia said. "And thanks. I'm—" She was still nervous around Dot and Dash, especially Dash. "I'm going to go, okay?"

"Happy snooping," Dash said.

Amelia looked right and left before crossing the street. She was checking for traffic—obviously—but she was also scanning to see if anyone in her family might be watching through one of the windows.

The coast looked clear.

"Come on, boy," she said to Doc, grateful to have him at her side. His presence made it bearable to have her mother as a suspect. Her only hope was that whatever she found in the shed would clear her mother's name.

They opened the gate slowly, to keep the squeak of the hinge down. The air felt thick and cool, and the sky was growing grayer by the minute. Rain was coming. That could make it tough for her dad to fix the roof.

Although she was on her family's own property, she was as jumpy as a sand flea. The shed was by the hedge. It was near where they'd first found Doc. He kept looking that way and tugging his leash.

"What is it?" she whispered.

He cocked his head and wagged his tail. She thought she understood—he was telling her that he remembered. Her heart welled with love.

Although crime was usually nonexistent in Urchin Beach, the MacGuffins kept their shed locked because bears sometimes wandered over from the woods, lured by the aroma of people's garbage and compost bins.

Amelia lifted the lock. It was a padlock, and her mom had the only key. But the detective book gave clear instructions on how to pick one.

Above all, be patient and do not force things. You have to will *the lock to open.*

You also needed two paper clips that had been bent just so, one to put tension on the bottom of the lock and another to pick the tumblers. Colin had done his best.

She realized she couldn't pick the lock and hold Doc's leash.

"Sit right here and be good, okay?" She set the leash in the dirt. Amelia slipped the first paper clip inside the lock and held it down with her fingers.

Doc looked as though he understood. She looked over her shoulder, toward the Morses' house. Dot and Dash waved from the second-story windows. She waved back.

Now came the moment of truth.

She slipped the second paper clip into the lock and wriggled, being patient and careful not to force anything. As she wiggled the paper clip against the pins, her world narrowed to include the lock, her two hands, and the paper clips in them. Rain started to fall. At first a drip here and a drip there, and then a steady patter of heavy drops that come from the kind of cloud that has both patience and a great deal of will.

At last there was a thrilling click. By then her back and shoulders were wet. But she didn't care. She'd done it. She looked up. The Morse twins were still watching. Dash made V-for-victory arms and Amelia nearly burst. She slipped the lock out of the hasp and put it in her pocket.

She opened the door. The shed smelled like it always did, of coffee grounds and spare gasoline, of dust, and of bags of potting soil. She stepped out of the rain. Slowly, patiently, and without forcing things, Amelia let her eyes adjust to the dim light.

Before long, she saw something that made her heart lurch. A large box. And then another. And another. All covered with sheets, as if locking them in the shed wasn't enough. As if they were things that needed to be hidden.

The rain came down harder, knocking against the roof in a

pattern that even Dash might find complicated. Amelia knew in her bones what it meant.

Take a step forward. Tear off the sheet. See what your mother has stashed in here. See what your mother doesn't want you to see. You must. It's your duty as a human being and as a detective.

Her hands, which had been so warm while they fiddled with the lock, were cold now. They felt as heavy as two buckets filled with wet sand. She took a breath and stepped forward. She reached for a cloth.

And that's when she heard her mother's voice behind her.

"Oh, Amelia. I wish you hadn't done that."

25

Something's Brewing

Amelia turned to face her mother. In the distance, she heard the Morse twins knocking. They'd been trying to warn her, but the sound of raindrops had swallowed the sounds of their tapping. Then she remembered Doc. He'd been sitting where her mother was standing. Now he wasn't.

"Oh no," she said. "DOC! COME BACK!"

"I asked you to stay out of the shed, Amelia," Mrs. MacGuffin said. "And now—oof!"

Mrs. MacGuffin lurched sideways. Doc must have heard the terror in Amelia's voice. He'd come running at top speed and had crashed into Mrs. MacGuffin, who was now sitting in a puddle.

Worse, Doc was not the clean and dry dog she'd taken on a walk. He was wet and extremely muddy. He shook his fur on Mrs. MacGuffin. This might have been a moment to ask for forgiveness in the Morse house, but in the MacGuffin house, that wouldn't be enough.

Mrs. MacGuffin pushed herself up and wiped her palms on her jeans. "First you're going to give him a bath while I change clothes. Then you're going to explain to me what you were doing in the shed. Those were supposed to be surprises for the festival."

Surprises for the festival. Amelia felt positively horrible.

When Amelia came downstairs with a clean and towel-dried dog, she found Mrs. MacGuffin sitting at the kitchen table drinking hot peppermint tea from one of the festive dragonfly mugs she'd brought home from the Pacific General Store. Her mother looked so disappointed, and Amelia wasn't sure whether it was because she'd ruined the surprise, gotten Mrs. MacGuffin muddy, or broken into the shed in the first place. Probably all three.

The shed did not contain the missing staff. Nor did it contain anything else that had gone missing . . . the half blankets, the toys, the jackets. The boxes contained booty of another sort, all bought legally and thoughtfully by Mrs. MacGuffin, who'd wanted to do something special for her family.

There was a carnival-style popcorn popper, a cotton candy machine, and a helium tank with a healthy supply of biodegradable balloons. She'd planned to give the three oldest MacGuffin children jobs working each of them during the Dragonfly Day Festival. After they'd earned back the cost, the rest of the money would be theirs to keep.

"If it makes the situation any better," Amelia said, "I was definitely surprised when I saw what was in there."

Mrs. MacGuffin rolled her eyes and laughed.

Bridget walked in. "Those new mugs look rad, even if the dragonfly on them makes me think of dead nymphs. I'm going to need some tea to soothe my weary heart."

"Amelia," Mrs. MacGuffin said, "will you please serve your sister tea?"

It seemed like a demand wearing the clothing of a polite request. In other words, not something she could say no to. Amelia wondered how long she'd have to be at her mother's beck and call for breaking into the shed. Probably between a long time and forever. Bridget was going to love it.

"Bridget," Mrs. MacGuffin said, "go get Colin. I have a surprise."

"A surprise?" Colin strode into the kitchen holding a clipboard.

"Is it a shovel?" Bridget asked. "A shovel of my very own?"

"It is not a shovel, Bridget. First you need to explain why you need your own shovel."

"I have my reasons," Bridget said. "Secret reasons."

"Colin," her mother said, ignoring Bridget, "would you also like some tea? Amelia is serving it."

He tapped his chapped lips with a finger. "Yes, I think I very much would."

Amelia set out a mug for each of them and then put dried peppermint leaves from their garden into two little bags. The minty scent wrapped itself around her and melted away the edges of her sorrows.

She brought the mugs to the table. "What's the clipboard for?"

"Oh, I was helping Dad with calculations about how much tar and how many shingles he needs for the roof. I find a clipboard is helpful when loose-leaf paper is the only option."

"What's the surprise if it's not a shovel?" Bridget asked. "Ow, Amelia! The tea is hot."

"I'll get you an ice cube," Colin said.

"You shouldn't have made it so hot," Bridget said.

"Tea is by definition hot," Amelia said.

"What about iced tea?" Bridget asked.

"Girls," Mrs. MacGuffin said.

When Colin returned with the ice, Mrs. MacGuffin told them about the surprise that Amelia had ruined.

"Dibs on the balloon station," Bridget said. "Biodegradable balloons are the smart choice for environmentalists like me."

"May I please be in charge of popcorn?" Colin said. "It's my favorite scent."

That left Amelia to operate the cotton candy machine, which felt like a dream come true. She wondered whether Dash liked cotton candy. Whether he'd be impressed by her skill at making cones of it, assuming that she could figure out how. Perhaps Miss Fortune had a book in the library.

"Mom," Bridget said, "you are the very greatest. I didn't know I wanted a balloon station almost as much as I want a shovel."

"Now we have to make sure the staircase is rebuilt so that the festival can happen," Mrs. MacGuffin said. "It's a shame that it's raining again. Wow, it's really coming down."

Amelia looked out the window at the silvery air and glistening hedge. "Are we still going to visit that address on the microchip?"

She hoped her mother would say no. That she'd changed her mind. That they didn't need to. That they could just keep Doc.

"As soon as I'm finished with my tea," Mrs. MacGuffin said.

"Can I blow up some practice balloons right now?" Bridget asked.

"I'd love to pop some corn," Colin said.

"Not yet, kids," Mrs. MacGuffin said. "The festival is three days off. That's hardly any time at all. You can wait."

Amelia could tell that three days seemed like a long time to Colin and Bridget. Not to her. If she didn't solve the case before then, well, she didn't know what to think. It seemed as though her mom had forgiven her. That was good.

"Amelia," Mrs. MacGuffin said. "Go get your raincoat and galoshes. We're going to take a drive."

Then again, maybe Mrs. MacGuffin hadn't.

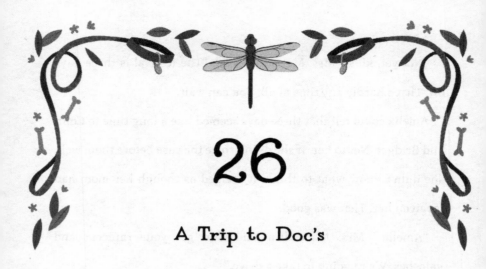

26

A Trip to Doc's

Mrs. MacGuffin eased the minivan onto the two-lane highway. The windshield wipers swung hard against the rain as they turned south, where the trees grew thicker and the homes more spread out.

"So," Mrs. MacGuffin said.

This was her technique. Mrs. MacGuffin would have made an excellent detective had she not chosen to be the co-owner of the Pacific General Store. The word *so* given to someone with a guilty conscience works like two paper clips that have been unfolded and reshaped into lock-picking tools. It puts the pressure on. It wiggles at the tumblers. It patiently and without force hangs in the air until the guilt springs forward.

"I was trying to solve a crime," Amelia said.

"What crime?"

"The Case of the Missing Dragonfly Staff," Amelia said.

"But why would the staff be in our shed? Who would have put it there? It's locked—only someone with a key could get in, and I have the sole key. Wait. How did *you* get in?"

Amelia wanted to fib. To claim it had been unlocked when she found it. But before she did, she considered a chapter she'd read in *How to Think Like a Master Detective*. Called "Lies, Liars, and Their Lying Ways," the chapter explained that you could trip up a suspect with a single lie. Amelia did not want to be caught in a lie. A girl caught in a lie would not be a girl likely to get to keep the extremely skinny dog she had grown to love. She didn't want to incriminate her brother, though.

She took a deep breath. "I didn't take your keys. I promise. I did take two paper clips, and I used them to open the lock." That was accurate, even if she'd left out Colin's role in shaping them.

"Where did you learn how to do that?" Her mother sounded impressed.

Amelia looked at Doc, who was looking out the rain-streaked window.

"From a book."

"Which book?"

"*How to Think Like a Master Detective*, by Edith Phipps, PhD."

"And you got this book—"

"From the library." Every single word of this was true.

"But why are you still looking for the staff? Dad found it on the beach." Mrs. MacGuffin glanced at Amelia in the rearview mirror.

"That's not the real one," Amelia said.

"How do you know?"

"I can feel it," Amelia said.

Her mother let out a big sigh. "Assuming this feeling of yours is correct, why did you think you would find it in our shed, of all places?"

"Because you told us not to look in there."

"But that would mean . . . that would mean . . ."

Amelia's eyes burned. She was going to cry. She stiffened her upper lip, but it did nothing, as she'd suspected. Her lower lip gave way.

And then her mother started laughing. It was not an unkind laugh, but it made things worse.

"Mom, stop it," Amelia said. "Please."

Between fits of laughter, Mrs. MacGuffin spoke. "I'm sorry for laughing. It's not at you. I promise. It's the thought that *I* might be a criminal . . . Shirl Locke is one of my best friends! I was voted Least Likely to Need a Lawyer in the high school yearbook. I am *honored* that you thought me capable of being a villain. This is the greatest thing that has happened to me in ages. Thank you, Amelia."

Amelia was so confused she had to stop crying. First, that people would vote for things like that in their yearbook. And second, that her mom was flattered to be a suspect. People were weird, grown-ups especially.

Mrs. MacGuffin eventually stopped laughing, shook her head, and said, "Oh, Amelia," and then, "Will you teach me how to pick a lock? That's so cool."

"Well, sure, okay, I guess," she said. "As long as you promise you're not going to go on a crime spree."

"I promise. I will use my newfound powers only for good," Mrs. MacGuffin said. "Like when people lose the key to their bicycle lock."

That sounded reasonable to Amelia. Then Doc whined and slid off the seat and sat on the carpeted floor of the van, leaning against her leg. She rubbed the velvet of his ears. "What's wrong, boy?"

"We're almost there," her mother said. "The turn's just ahead."

Could Doc have known where they were? It was possible. Dogs were supposed to have an excellent sense of smell.

Her mother put on the turn signal, slowed, and turned into a gravel road lined high with trees. PRIVATE LANE, a sign read.

"Are you sure we should be doing this?" Amelia asked.

"Absolutely," Mrs. MacGuffin said. "If Doc belongs to these people, the right thing to do is take him home. Otherwise, it's stealing. And you know me. I am most definitely *not* a thief."

Amelia made a noise of agreement. It was the best she could do. Part of her wished her mother *had* been a criminal, because then they could have kept Doc without driving down this creepy private lane to do the right thing. At least it was pretty. The green was intense, smudged, and heavy with rainwater. It felt as though she were inside a painting.

They reached the house. It was small and dingy white with peeling green shutters, set in the middle of a grassy clearing. The grass looked shaggy and neglected. Mrs. MacGuffin parked and turned off the engine. Right away, raindrops made it hard to see out.

"Do you think anyone's home?" Amelia asked.

"I can't tell," Mrs. MacGuffin said.

The lights were off. There were no cars parked in the driveway. A stillness to the place suggested it had been empty for a while. It felt creepy—or worse.

"Do you want to stay in the car?" Mrs. MacGuffin asked.

Amelia did. She very much did. Knocking on the door of a strange house was bad enough. But a strange house with a sinister vibe? And then knowing that she might have to hand over Doc to whoever lived there? No thanks.

But it didn't seem fair to make her mom brave the rain and looming danger all by herself. Least Likely to Need a Lawyer in high school meant she was law-abiding and probably as anxious as Amelia.

"I'll come with," she said.

"I suppose we should bring Doc too," Mrs. MacGuffin said.

"Yeah, I guess we should."

It was all happening so quickly. Amelia didn't feel ready. The leash was coiled in her lap. She clipped it to Doc's collar. He whined, a soft curlicue of noise that she might have missed had she not been listening so carefully.

She pushed the button to open the side door. There was a clunk and then the sliding sound and a gust of warm, wet air that smelled of pine needles. Doc cowered by the other door. She stepped out, holding the leash gently.

"Come on, boy," she said.

Doc wouldn't budge. Mrs. MacGuffin peered into the van.

"Huh," she said. "He didn't mind getting out of the car at the vet's."

"I don't want to make him," Amelia said.

"Neither do I. Tell you what. You hop back in. Wait with Doc. I'll see if anybody's home."

Her mother approached the house. She looked so brave and yet she was not a big woman at all. Many middle schoolers were already taller. Amelia scooted closer to Doc, who leaned against the far door and shivered. She buried her hand in his fur and told him that everything would be okay. She was saying it as much for herself as she was for him.

Her mother knocked and then stepped back. A minute passed. Her mother knocked again. She waited. She peeked through a window. She looked at Amelia and shrugged. And then something seemed to catch her eye—a big-leaf maple tree growing about twenty feet from the house. Amelia leaned forward for a better view.

Her mother crouched at the base of the tree and lifted something from the grass. A rope. It was stained green with moss and pollen, but Amelia could see two details that gave her quite a bit of information: the rope was knotted around the tree, and its end had been severed roughly—as if it had been chewed off.

Her mother made her thinking face. And even though Mrs. MacGuffin had not had the benefit of reading *How to Think Like a Master Detective*, Amelia knew her mother well enough to know they were thinking along the same lines.

That was a tree that a dog had been tied to. And even though Doc did not have a rope around his neck when they found him, it seemed likely that he'd been the dog tied to the tree. That would explain why he didn't want to get out of the car. Why he had whined so delicately.

Doc was afraid. He was afraid he was being returned to a place where he'd been tied to a tree, which was no way for a dog—or anyone—to be treated.

There was a crunch of wheels on gravel. A truck was approaching. Amelia had a hunch who it was. Doc's owners, returning. They parked the truck behind the MacGuffin van.

Even if Amelia and her mother had wanted to leave—which Amelia for sure did—they couldn't. They were blocked in.

27

The Bearded Stranger

Mrs. MacGuffin hurried to the van. She stood between the stranger and the open door.

"Can I help you?" the stranger asked. He was tall and stooped forward, like a question mark. He wore a raincoat with the hood pulled up. Even so, rainwater dripped from his long beard.

"Close the door, Amelia," her mother said.

Amelia didn't want to, in case her mother needed defending. But she did as she was told.

She watched the two adults talk and tried to make sense of their body language and gestures. Beside her, Doc trembled so hard his tag jingled. What were they saying? Amelia felt like a log bobbing in the ocean—adrift, far from home, and waiting to be caught by a wave that would return it to shore. She couldn't stand it. Someone had to fight for Doc. She opened the door again. She forced herself to speak, and the voice that came out barely sounded like hers.

"Doc doesn't like it here. He doesn't even want to get out of the van. What if they tie him up again? What if—"

Her mom held up a hand. "It's all right, Amelia. This is Mr. Gottfred. He's not Doc's owner. Let's go home. We'll need to think things through."

Doc leaned against Amelia as they drove home, and her mother recounted the conversation she'd had with Mr. Gottfred. He'd worked for the people who lived there, doing odd jobs around the house and property, and he'd come to collect a paycheck one day, but no one was home. He figured they'd be back because Doc was tied to the tree. He'd returned, and by then Doc was gone.

"He'd had no idea they'd left Doc behind," she said. "Apparently his owners called him Charlie Mayfield."

At the sound of the name, Doc wagged the tip of his tail.

"Well, he's Doc now," Amelia said. Doc wagged harder, and that felt like something. Like he knew he belonged with them. That he was safe. That he wasn't Charlie Mayfield anymore. He wasn't a dog tied up to a tree. He was a dog who lived inside with a family. A dog who had a collar and a leash and several toys and separate bowls for food and water.

She waited for her mom to say something, anything, that would affirm that Doc was now theirs for sure.

But she didn't.

"I could get a job," Amelia said. "And I'd help pay for his food and his vet bills and everything."

"Oh, Amelia," her mother said. "A dog is a lot of responsibility, and so is having five kids and a store and an old house where everything breaks all the time. I don't see how we can afford him without finding hundreds of extra dollars in the budget. I wish we could. But we can't. We just can't. And as much as I love your initiative, I'm afraid there aren't real jobs for kids your age."

Amelia swallowed hard. She knew this was true. She also knew that Doc needed a home. And that she and her siblings loved him.

"I thought love was more powerful than luck," she said. "I thought love was always enough." It was surprisingly hard getting the words out, as if she was prying open an oyster to get at whatever was inside.

If love wasn't enough, then Amelia would have to change everything she believed about the world.

"I'll talk to your dad," her mother said. "But please don't get your hopes up. It's too hard on me."

Not as hard as this is on Doc, Amelia thought.

And then they were home. Only it didn't feel like the same home she'd left. There was the porch. The mailbox. The fence. There was the turret. A window of the room she shared with Bridget. Amelia looked up, and the rain spattered her face.

"Doc," she called.

This time, he got out of the car, his tail wagging, his tongue out. She wanted to tell him, once more, that everything would be okay. But she didn't know that was the case. She didn't know that they'd get to keep him.

Amelia stroked his head now damp with rain, and they walked up the porch steps behind her mother, knowing that the house felt different because she was different. Less certain. Sadder. She'd made no progress in solving the Case of the Missing Dragonfly Staff. She had no more clues. No clues, no hunches, no hope. There were fewer than three days left before the festival.

If love wasn't enough, if luck was gone, what would become of them all?

Urchin Beach Staircase Halfway Finished

by Birdie Wheeler, News Intern

A group of intrepid volunteers led by Pacific General Store co-owner Dave MacGuffin has completed part of the staircase-rebuilding project.

"We're halfway finished," MacGuffin said, "which is the same thing as being halfway unfinished, but I'm choosing to be optimistic about this. Wouldn't you rather have a half-full bucket than a half-empty one?"

Not everyone else in town shares MacGuffin's "bucket half-full" view.

"If this rain keeps up," local Realtor Mike Jung said, "they're never going to finish."

Heavy rain is predicted for the next several days in Urchin Beach. Two days remain until the Dragonfly Day Festival—the first time we can expect to see sun, according to a forecast from the National Weather Service.

"I insist on a bucket-half-full approach," MacGuffin said with a shrug when a journalist told him of the gloomy forecast.

"Sounds about right," Jung said. "Dave has a bucket half-full of something gross, like banana slugs. Who wants those?"

Bridget MacGuffin, who happened to be in the room with her father, informed Jung that many creatures would enjoy a half bucket of banana slugs: raccoons, ducks, geese, and garter snakes, to name a few. She further informed Jung that banana slugs might be moist and sticky but that they help forest duff decompose.

"Unlike you," she said.

Jung replied, "Every single one of those animals is gross, Miss MacGuffin. Slugs are slimy rotters. A garter snake pooped on my hands when I was a boy. It smelled like whoa. There's a reason they call raccoons trash pandas. And don't even get me started on ducks and geese. They'd better scurry. Besides, none of that changes the fact that Urchin Beach is in trouble. The town ought to make the mayor wear a hat that says, 'Vote for Someone Else Next Time.'"

In response, Mayor Miranda Hoffman said, "I don't wear hats, as everyone who knows me knows."

In more positive news, it appears that conditions are improved at the slough where dragonfly eggs hatch into nymphs, and from which the nymphs emerge in their full glory as green darner dragonflies. Much of the flooding has receded. University of Puget Sound biologist Beryl Bernina said she had inspected the region and liked what she saw.

"It looks as though some restoration has occurred," she said, "although it is unclear who has performed the work. But there just might be some *Anax junius* hatching here yet. That's a green darner dragonfly, in case your Latin skills aren't the best."

28

The Rain Came Down

There are tales of rain that flooded the earth. Rain that fell for days and weeks. Rain that left puddles that became lakes that scratched their chins and considered becoming oceans.

Amelia felt as though she'd been dropped into one of those stories. Two days had passed since she and her mom had driven to Doc's house. There was still no sign of his owners. There was still no agreement from Mr. and Mrs. MacGuffin that Doc could stay. Doc also kept sneaking out of the backyard and coming home muddy. So did Bridget. Amelia thought the two of them were running off together for fun, but Bridget denied it, and when Amelia called her a liar, Bridget burst into tears and locked her out of their room, which made Amelia feel sick to her stomach.

Meanwhile, Amelia gave Doc bath after bath, but that had meant a lot of dirty towels and a lot of dirty looks from her parents.

Maybe it was the rain. Maybe it was the loss of the staff. But everyone was in a crabby mood. The twins were crabby because they didn't have their blanket halves. Bridget was crabby for reasons she wouldn't discuss. Amelia was crabby because Bridget didn't want to talk to her and refused to admit she'd gotten Doc muddy. Colin wasn't crabby, but that's because he was worried about everyone else, and he only ever liked to experience one emotion at a time.

One day remained before the Dragonfly Day Festival. The newspaper headlines made Amelia's palms feel clammy as she read them over breakfast.

Thefts Continue. Authorities Stumped

No Dragonfly Nymphs Spotted Despite Anonymous Habitat Restoration Efforts

But it wasn't just the MacGuffin moods that were in the dumps. When Amelia stopped at the library to return her books, Miss Fortune actually unzipped Amelia's backpack and gave it a thorough inspection. This had never happened before. It was humiliating.

"I can't take any chances," Miss Fortune said. "Not with all the thefts in town."

When Miss Fortune checked in the books again, she held up *How to Think Like a Master Detective.* "Was the book too grown-up for you? I was afraid of that."

"No!" Amelia said, stung by the idea that the book was too hard for her. "It was useless. I can't believe that the library doesn't have anything better."

Miss Fortune stood with her mouth open. Amelia froze for a minute. That's how long it took for her to be able to apologize.

"I didn't mean that," she said. "The book—the book was helpful."

Miss Fortune looked so sad. But Amelia was too ashamed to admit that she'd tried and failed. That she'd made an investigation wall and had scrutinized suspects, their motives, and the clues they'd left behind. She'd done her best and it wasn't good enough, which made everything worse. Maybe if she hadn't tried, she wouldn't feel so terrible.

She slunk away without even saying thank-you or goodbye.

Then at Clyde's, where Amelia went to pick up some grapes for the toddlers, Clyde yelled at her for getting close to the peaches. "Those are fragile," he said. "If you bruise them, you buy them."

Bonnie wasn't in the yarn shop, but she'd stuck a sign in the window. BACK IN 10 MINUTES. DON'T STEAL ANYTHING, YOU JERKS.

On the sidewalk, she passed Eugenides, Hayden, and Kat, who

was wearing her roller derby gear. They were arguing over the location of the flying disc they used for their Ultimate Frisbee games.

"You should have put it someplace safe," Hayden told Kat.

"I wasn't the last to have it," Kat said. "I let Eugenides have it. Remember that time he stole erasers in kindergarten?"

"That was a long time ago," Eugenides said. "I couldn't help it. I thought erasers shaped like food were so cool, and my mom wouldn't buy any for me."

"Well, now we can't play Ultimate anymore." Hayden shoved Kat backward on her skates, and she crashed into a fire hydrant.

This wasn't the Urchin Beach Amelia knew. Usually everyone in the town was friendly. Cheerful. People didn't call one another jerks. They didn't suspect others of stealing, let alone damaging fruit willy-nilly. And they didn't shove each other into fire hydrants. This was what happened, though, when people didn't trust one another. When they didn't give the benefit of the doubt. When they didn't assume that everyone had good intentions.

That was what the thief really had stolen. It wasn't so much the loss of flying discs and jackets and decorations or even precious blanket halves. It was a sense of safety and goodwill. The idea that everyone cared about everyone else, that everyone could trust everyone else.

And Amelia was out of time. The countdown sign for the Dragonfly Day Festival had the number 1 hanging below it.

Things inside the MacGuffin home hadn't improved while Amelia was out. Mr. MacGuffin had spent all week trying to fix the beach stairs. But he hadn't had enough volunteers, so they still weren't finished. Mrs. MacGuffin was running the store all by herself. Both parents came home tired and grumpy, and Mr. MacGuffin muttered about not having a chance to fix the roof, which meant the kids had to empty the leak buckets several times a day.

When they forgot one time, Maya snapped at them because water was all over the floor of the turret. Maya had never, not once, snapped at them.

She was so upset by it that she burst into tears and wept until her nose was red. Duncan and Emma got the sympathy weepies, and soon everyone felt the worst they ever had. Then Maya apologized to all the kids. Bridget wasn't there to hear it, though. She was gone, as usual. It felt as if Bridget didn't even want to be a MacGuffin anymore—as though they weren't just on narrow paths, they were on different paths altogether.

"Not even poetry can fix this," Maya said.

Amelia knew what could. Solving the crime. Catching the thief who'd taken so much from all of them. But it was too hard. She'd failed.

That night, Amelia was trying to teach Doc tricks in front of the fire. It wasn't going well. No matter what she asked him to do, he wouldn't. Not even for treats. He kept stealing them from her fingertips and then wagging his tail so she couldn't possibly be disappointed in him.

She lay on her back and let out a noise of pure frustration. Doc rolled over on his back and moaned.

Then her father crouched next to them. "Hard day, Bedelia?"

He hadn't called her that since she was little.

"You could say that." Doc sat up and put his chin on Mr. MacGuffin's shoulder, and Mr. MacGuffin made a goofy face and gave him a scratch.

"It'll get better," Mr. MacGuffin said. "But I'm here if you want to talk."

She did and she didn't. She wasn't sure where to begin and what to include. And part of her didn't want anyone, even her well-meaning dad, to dismiss what she was feeling by saying it would get better. It wouldn't. She wasn't wrong. She knew it. Her failure to solve the crime had let down the whole town. Dragonfly Day was going to be a disaster. Things would only get worse from there.

Before this, she hadn't really believed that the dragonfly staff was lucky. She'd wanted it to be, the way you want to believe gnomes build little houses in the woods and leprechauns hoard pots of gold where rainbows end. Now she wasn't so sure. The disappearance of the staff had been the first domino in a cascade of misfortunes. The best explanation was that the staff had been lucky and now all that luck was gone.

Her father stood. "I could use some cocoa. So how about this. You make us some while I dry off a bit. Then the two of us can talk by the fire."

29

Cocoa and Frustration

It turned out Mr. MacGuffin was not the only one who wanted cocoa. It also turned out that Bridget and Mrs. MacGuffin had made a batch of shortbread while Colin kept an eye on the twins. Doc whined to go out, so Amelia let him.

"Don't get too muddy," she warned.

Amelia made enough cocoa for everyone, and Mr. MacGuffin suggested the younger MacGuffins take theirs up to the turret and read stories to the twins while he and Amelia talked.

Mr. MacGuffin put their cocoa and shortbread on a tray and carried it to the coffee table in front of the fireplace. Instead of sitting in chairs, they sat on the floor, one on each end of the table. It was a cozy way to sit and have a snack, and in ordinary times, Amelia might even have felt lucky.

These were not ordinary times.

"Tell me all your troubles," Mr. MacGuffin said.

Amelia exhaled. Where to begin?

"I'm worried about the town," she said.

"The town's an awfully big thing for a person to worry about all alone," Mr. MacGuffin said.

She was glad he hadn't said it was a big thing for a little kid to worry about. She wasn't that little anymore, and she was as capable of worry as someone much larger.

"I can't help it," she said. "So many unlucky things have happened since the dragonfly staff went missing."

"But it's back," Mr. MacGuffin said. "I found it at the beach."

Amelia didn't want to contradict him or hurt his feelings.

"It feels to me," she said, "as if the town's luck has gone away. Everyone is crabby. People are suspicious of one another. We're being mean. With all these bad feelings, I don't see how we can have fun on Dragonfly Day—if we even get any dragonflies at all because of the flooding."

Mr. MacGuffin took a sip of his cocoa. He rubbed his beard, as if to let Amelia know he was thinking.

"The town's been here for a hundred years," he said. "The store, almost that long."

"But that's because of the luck," she said.

"Sure, there's always luck involved," Mr. MacGuffin said. "But there's also work. And cooperation. And looking out for one another. That's not luck. It's a choice. It's never been about the dragonfly staff. It's always been the choice each one of us makes to love. There is no greater magic than that."

"It's not a choice. People *have* to do that," Amelia said.

"Oh, Amelia, but that's the thing. They don't."

"Why do they, then?" Amelia asked.

"Love," Mr. MacGuffin said. "That's what love is, making that choice."

Amelia considered her father's words. She breathed in the sweetness of cocoa and the shortbread cookies that her mom hadn't had to make, but she had. And she knew why. For love. Even so, it didn't feel like enough.

"I wanted to solve the crime," Amelia said. "I wanted to find out who stole the dragonfly staff so we could make things like they used to be. I miss the way things used to be."

"Change happens all the time," Mr. MacGuffin said. "Whether we like it or not."

Amelia scowled. This change didn't happen. It was caused. "The thief has to pay for all of this."

"I understand what you're feeling," her father said. "And I also understand your desire to help. You're smart. You're resourceful.

You have integrity. The dragonfly staff means something to us. It's a reminder, most of all, that we're lucky to be here. Lucky to have one another. I can see why you're disappointed that you weren't the one to find it."

It's still missing, she wanted to say. *You found a regular old stick. This isn't disappointment. It's rage.* Instead, she took a bite of shortbread.

"And here's the thing about crime," Mr. MacGuffin continued. "Sometimes people take things without knowing they're important. Sometimes people take things because they need them. Sometimes it's because they're hurting or even angry. So, even though it feels good to find out who did something that hurt us, you can't know what to think about someone until you have all the facts."

There was nothing about that in *How to Think Like a Master Detective.* As far as the book was concerned, once a crime was solved, that was that. There was nothing in there to say what to do when people *thought* a crime had been solved but it hadn't. There was also nothing in there that said some crimes might not be what they appeared to be. The book made it seem as though crimes were puzzles to solve, and in doing so, one could repair the broken world.

Amelia sipped her cocoa. Outside, the sky bulged with iron clouds and looked nothing like a world that had been fixed.

"Well, what about Doc?" she asked. Mr. and Mrs. MacGuffin still hadn't decided whether Doc got to stay, or whether they were fostering him for the time being.

Mr. MacGuffin started to speak, and Amelia knew he was going to say something like, "What about him?"

She set down her cocoa and crossed her arms.

Mr. MacGuffin's expression softened. "A dog is a lot of responsibility, Amelia."

"I know! I've given him six baths already!"

"It's not just that," he said. "It's the feeding and the walking—"

"We're all helping with that. We like doing it!"

"—and it's things like the vet. Doc was malnourished. We don't know what happened in his medical history and whether he has special needs. We don't know—"

"He's not less of a dog just because someone treated him badly." She picked fur off her jeans. Gray, black, reddish, and white. Every color for a dog who was everything to her.

"Dad, please." She couldn't stop tears from running down her face. Even if she'd had lips made of steel, she wouldn't have been able to keep them stiff. "I thought looking out for one another was important."

"It is, it is," Mr. MacGuffin said, his voice soft. "But we have to look out for ourselves too."

"I need him, Dad," Amelia said.

Mr. MacGuffin drank the last of his cocoa. "Well, you should probably let him inside. He's barking."

She opened the back door and there was Doc, wagging his tail as though he'd been gone for weeks and was thrilled to see her. He was muddy again, all the way up to his knees, and the fur on his belly looked like a cake that had been frosted by a toddler.

"Oh, buddy," she said.

From behind her, her father's voice: "I'll get the bathtub running. But for now, Amelia, can we table the discussion of where Doc's forever home is? There's a lot to do before tomorrow, and Mom and I really need to keep our eyes on the prize."

Doc is the prize, she wanted to say. But she didn't. She knew what he meant, and she was part of the family and part of the community, and she was going to do her best to contribute.

If only she could figure out who'd stolen the real staff, where they'd taken it, and get it back in time for the festival. Everything would feel right again, even if the luck of the staff was in their heads. But at this point, it seemed impossible.

"Of course, Dad," she said.

She led Doc upstairs for bath number seven.

30

Dragonfly Day Festival at Last

Amelia woke the next morning to a robin's-egg sky. She raced to the window of the turret. Bridget was already there, with Doc sitting next to her, his clean fur gleaming in the brilliant light.

"You can see all the way to the beach," Bridget said. "It's a miracle."

Amelia knew what Bridget meant—that at last the rain was gone.

It felt good to talk with her sister again. They'd hardly spoken all week, and Amelia supposed that rift had made her bad feelings worse. She held Bridget's hand the way she used to. Bridget gave her three squeezes for *I love you*. Amelia almost made a joke about Bridget's dirty fingernails, but she decided not to ruin a nice moment. She squeezed back four times, and Bridget smiled.

They peered down together and saw the freshly built staircase, its new wood pale and lovely against the bluff. Mr. MacGuffin's team had awakened early and pounded in the last treads before dawn. The mayor was also on the beach, helping set up the platform where she would make her big speech. Officer Shirley Locke was there as well. It made Amelia feel good that someone was keeping an eye out for crime.

The Morse twins were awake too. Dot was in her window, waving. Dash was in his, and he'd spelled out a coded message.

-.-- .- -.-- --..-- / ... ..- -.

Amelia pulled out the translation guide she'd checked out of the library.

She turned to Bridget. "It says, 'YAY, SUN.'"

"I know," Bridget said.

Did she? If so, Amelia was envious. She'd been hoping to learn it and impress Dash, and here Bridget was ahead of her. Maybe that was what she'd been doing when she was off by herself.

Still, Amelia's mood felt bright. It might have been the sun. It might have been knowing that Dragonfly Day had arrived at last. That she could finally release the heavy block of dread she'd been dragging behind her. Within hours, the road leading into town would be full of hopeful tourists, and maybe the sight of them would be enough to snap the town out of its funk. And it didn't hurt that Dash Morse had made a message for his window. All the evidence pointed to the fact that he was treating her as a friend. Imagine that!

She and Bridget dressed and bounded down the stairs. Colin was making breakfast, his specialty—toast and a choice of honey butter or jam. The twins were in their high chairs, dipping toast fingers into jam.

Doc yipped to go out, so Amelia ushered him into the backyard. "Don't get dirty, bud."

"He's going to get dirty," Bridget said. "He keeps going into the hedge. I think he's dug a fort in there."

Doc did like the hedge, but Amelia thought it was because that was where they'd found him. She imagined that he liked reliving the memory. Doc's uncertain fate wound up her insides again. She had that full-of-springs feeling she got when she wasn't sure how things were going to turn out. Life didn't work like a book, unfortunately. You couldn't flip ahead and see what happened to make things bearable. You had to grit it out one minute at a time.

Tomorrow. She'd ask then for a final answer on Doc's fate.

"Your toast is served," Colin announced.

The three eldest MacGuffin children ate at the table while the toddlers babbled to each other and put wet strips of toast in each other's mouths. It was disgusting, but since they were twins, they already had pretty much the same slobber.

"I'm really looking forward to manning the popcorn machine," Colin said.

"'Manning' it." Bridget scoffed. "You're eight."

Amelia didn't like it when Bridget teased Colin. "It's an expression, Bridget. He could hardly have said 'childing' it."

"Whatever. I want to see how many balloons it takes to make Duncan and Emma fly," Bridget said.

Amelia blanched. "No! That could get out of control! And besides, you're supposed to be *selling* the balloons. We have to cover the cost of the equipment."

"But levitating toddlers would be an attraction we could charge extra for," Bridget said.

"Who's talking about levitating toddlers?" Mrs. MacGuffin walked in and made herself a plate of food.

Bridget, Colin, and Amelia took simultaneous bites of toast so they wouldn't have to answer.

"I didn't think anyone would say anything quite so silly as that," Mrs. MacGuffin said. "To be clear, you will not levitate the twins, today, tomorrow, or any other day."

"Except in case of quicksand," Bridget said. "Then you would be a fool to say no to the lifting powers of helium."

"I'll keep that in mind," Mrs. MacGuffin said.

"Do I smell toast?" That was Mr. MacGuffin, who was trying to walk and tie his bow tie at the same time.

"Here," Mrs. MacGuffin said. She finished tying the knot, and Amelia got a warm feeling looking at her parents looking at each other.

Woof.

That was Doc, wanting to come in. She opened the door and dunked each of his paws into a bucket of water kept there expressly for that purpose. Then she towel dried him. "Who is a good boy? Who is the best boy for not getting muddy?"

Doc licked her face. He was the best boy, and he knew it. There was zero mystery attached to that.

"Who's ready to see the first dragonfly of the year?" asked Mr. MacGuffin.

All five MacGuffin children spoke at once.

"Me!"

"Me!"

"Me!"

"Me!"

"Me!"

Doc woofed.

That would be something, Amelia thought, if one of them did. It would mean $1,000. Surely that was enough that they could keep Doc.

"Then let's go," Mrs. MacGuffin said.

31

Sounds Like Heartbreak

The popcorn popper, balloon inflater, and cotton candy machine were already loaded into the minivan by the time everyone made it outside.

"Dot and Dash helped us," Mrs. MacGuffin said. "Such nice kids."

"We would have helped," Amelia said.

"The Morses have middle school muscles," Bridget said.

"I'll be in middle school in a few weeks," Amelia said.

"Better start pumping iron, then," Bridget said. Then she laughed. Amelia did too. And she flexed her biceps.

"Like one of Clyde's cantaloupes," Bridget said.

They decided to set up on the small, grassy field near the top of the stairs. The popcorn maker and the cotton candy machine needed to be plugged in, and the van had a real working outlet near the rear seat, and Colin had attached it to a power strip so that everyone had the electricity they needed.

Mrs. MacGuffin took the twins and Doc to the swings so they wouldn't get underfoot while everyone else unloaded equipment. The whole town was doing a variation of this. Bonnie was getting ready to sell knitting kits. Clyde had made row after row of fruit baskets. Kat Bacon's mother was setting up her tarot booth—everyone did something to make things fun for tourists, who would arrive in droves before long.

Amelia felt as excited as she had in days. Maybe everything would work out. Maybe it would be okay. The mayor spotted them and waved. She always wore a suit, but today, she had on her special one, navy blue with white stars. She also had her keys on a lanyard that read URCHIN BEACH REALTY: MAKING THE DREAM REAL WITH MIKE JUNG. Mr. Jung stood nearby with a miniature rose in his buttonhole and a hat that read VOTE HOFFMAN.

"If it isn't the MacGuffins!" The mayor held up the dragonfly staff—well, the fake one—and gave it a little shake.

"Hello, Mayor Hoffman," Mr. MacGuffin said.

"Is that popcorn?" the mayor asked.

"Not yet," Colin said. "It's kernels and oil."

"I love popcorn," the mayor said.

"We also have future helium balloons and cotton candy," Bridget said.

"Fantastic," the mayor said. "This will be our best Dragonfly Day Festival yet. Once the PA system is set up, we can start the parade music. And then tourists should arrive soon with their beautiful wallets. Keep an eye peeled for green darner dragonflies, kids! First one's worth a thousand dollars!"

The mayor walked off, her arm linked with Mr. Jung's.

"Let's get this show on the road," Mr. MacGuffin said.

"But I thought we'd agreed to set it up on this field," Colin said. "The road seems risky."

"It's an expression," Amelia said.

"Thank you for explaining," Colin said.

"I'm all set up," Bridget said. She'd unfolded a card table, opened the box of biodegradable balloons, and set the helium tank next to her station. "Check out my sign."

She unrolled a banner that read URCHIN BEACH BALLOONS: IT'S HIGH TIME YOU BOUGHT ONE. Beneath that, in smaller lettering, it read THESE AREN'T BAD FOR BIRDS OR FISH. —BRIDGET MACGUFFIN, PROPRIETOR.

"That looks terrific, Bridget," Mr. MacGuffin said. "And I tip my hat in the direction of your pun. It's funny because it's about the helium that makes the balloons float."

Bridget gave her dad a good-humored dead-eyed stare. "Can I be the first to use the stairs to the beach? There's something I want to check out."

"Well," Mr. MacGuffin said.

"Please," Bridget said.

"Off you go," he said, "but come back soon. The tourists will arrive in the next half hour or so."

Bridget scampered down the stairs, shouting, "First! First! First!"

Amelia looked at her dad, who put a finger to his lips and shook his head. "She doesn't need to know others have already used the stairs."

"I won't tell a soul," Colin said.

Amelia smiled until she heard a voice behind her.

"Tell a soul what?" Dash Morse hopped off his bike.

"Sorry, Dash, sworn to secrecy," Colin said.

Dot skidded up next. "Found you guys. When will the popcorn be ready?"

"We have to set up the machines first," Amelia said.

"Want help?" Dash asked.

"Does a green darner dragonfly have six legs?" Colin said.

"That means yes," Amelia said.

"I can help too," Dot said. "Dibs on setting up popcorn. Dibs on first bag."

"Have at it," Dash said. "Cotton candy is my favorite."

Soon the machines were set up along with signs. Colin's read TOP POP IN URCHIN BEACH. Amelia's read SWEETEST SUNSETS.

"Do you think people will get it?" she asked Dash.

He pinched a tuft of cotton candy and stuffed it into his mouth. "I think it's genius. And this is delicious. Did you know in England that they call it candy floss?"

Colin giggled. "I wouldn't mind flossing my teeth with this."

"This is the best popcorn I've ever had," Dot said.

"And if a kernel gets stuck, you can floss it out." Colin laughed so hard he had to bend double, and this made Dash and Dot laugh too.

Amelia had almost forgotten how great it was to be surrounded by laughter. It was maybe the way the sugar in the cotton candy machine felt as you twirled a paper cone through it—like you were a lonely, single grain being swept into a wondrous galaxy.

Music started: the kind of song you could march to. It wasn't Amelia's favorite kind of music, full of brass instruments and booming drums. But she couldn't deny that it made her feel like joining a parade of people walking from the beach through the town and back again. Her knees tingled. Her feet found the beat. Soon she and Colin and Dot and Dash were jumping around yelling, "Sunsets for sale! Popcorn for sale!"

All the heaviness she'd carried during the rainy days was evaporating the way puddles do in sunlight. Everything was going to be okay. In that moment, she knew it. How could anything bad happen in a town everyone loved so much, with neighbors who felt like family? And Amelia meant that part. They did feel like family. And sometimes, families need to work to understand one another, and it's work they do because of love. Maybe that's what her parents meant when they said love was enough. Maybe love can't put food on the table. Maybe it can't fix a leaky roof. But it's the fuel that keeps you trying to make sure everyone has everything they need.

"Should we bring a tiny cloud of cotton candy to the twins?" Dash asked. "We passed them on the way here. Your dog was licking their feet every time they hit the high point on the swing."

Amelia nodded. She and Dash each made a miniature puff of it. Duncan and Emma didn't need anything more than that. As they walked to the swings, a familiar voice called Amelia's name.

It was Delphine, and she and Birdie were holding hands and running toward her.

She handed Dash the tiny cone of cotton candy just in time to be sandwiched in an enormous Delphine-Birdie hug.

"Ahhhhk!" Amelia made a noise like a startled bird and looked up at Delphine, whose long black hair was in two braids. Her glasses were smudged as usual. Amelia didn't realize how much she'd missed Delphine until they were together again.

"You have to tell me all about being an oceanographer," Amelia said.

"Birdie showed me her articles," Delphine said. "So rad. What did you do when I was gone?"

"Well," Amelia said. She didn't want to say that she'd failed to solve a mystery and gotten into what felt like a fight with Bridget. "We got a—" She was going to say "temporary dog," but Dash strolled up.

"She got new neighbors is what," Dash said. He introduced himself to Delphine.

"I already know everything about him," Birdie said. "On account of that article I wrote when they moved in."

"Well, maybe not everything," Dash said.

Amelia almost died for how mysterious he could be. She could tell that Delphine was impressed too, because she said "Wa sai" very quietly. Delphine was fluent in Mandarin. And thanks to Delphine, Amelia knew *wa sai* meant "wow."

"We were just bringing this cotton candy to the twins," Amelia said.

"Where did you get that?" Birdie asked.

"Mom got us machines," Amelia said. "Popcorn, cotton candy, and helium balloons."

"I want one of everything," Delphine said.

"Amelia," Birdie said, "you should have told me. I could have had a scoop in the paper."

"Tell Colin to give you popcorn on the house," Amelia said. "Wait, no. Tell him that he shouldn't charge you for it. He'll understand that better."

Delphine and Birdie, who'd spent plenty of time with Colin, laughed.

Just then, there was a cracking noise in the distance. It sounded like popcorn. Then like giant logs being tapped against one another. Then came a low rumble that did not stop.

"What was that?" Delphine asked.

"Sounds like a news story," Birdie said.

"Sounds like a mudslide," Dash said.

To Amelia, it sounded like heartbreak.

The friends looked at one another, and in an instant, they decided without using words or even secret codes. In another instant, they were running side by side to the town square.

32

The End of the Road

By the time they reached the town square, the rumbling had stopped. The people of Urchin Beach had gathered, arriving on foot, on bicycle, in strollers. The mayor stood on a podium in front of Glenda, holding the fake staff. No one spoke, not even the twins.

There was something about the sound: Even though Amelia had never heard anything like it, she knew it was terrible.

"Mayor?" Mr. MacGuffin said. "Are you all right?"

The mayor was most definitely not all right. She dropped the staff, removed her glasses, and covered her eyes.

"That was a mudslide," she said. "I'd know the sound anywhere."

A mudslide. Dash had been right. But where had it happened? Had anyone been hurt?

Officer Locke sped up in her mobile crime unit. She stopped abruptly and hopped out.

"A mudslide . . . has blocked . . . the road," she panted. "Nobody's . . . going to be able . . . to get here . . . today. The . . . only . . . good news is . . . it missed all the cars. We got . . . lucky."

It was good news indeed that no one had been hurt. Maybe even lucky. But this development was otherwise disastrous. That was it for Dragonfly Day. If tourists couldn't get there, Urchin Beachers wouldn't raise the money they needed. This was bad for everyone. Bad for the town. The financial hardship to come meant they'd have to give up Doc.

Urchin Beach residents stood around the mayor, their mouths open, their eyes wide with shock and dismay. Bonnie. Clyde. Mr. King. Miss Fortune. Eugenides, Kat, Hayden. Delphine and her mom and dad, Birdie, her parents, and her two siblings.

Amelia had let every one of these people down. The shame of it felt like another mudslide but one that tore up her insides.

Colin sidled up.

"Where's Doc?" he asked.

Amelia looked around frantically. She called his name. She couldn't see him. He didn't come. That wasn't all. The staff was gone.

Stolen.

Stolen.

And that's when she knew everything that she needed to know about the town thief.

Amelia recalled a passage she'd read at the end of *How to Think Like a Master Detective*:

The moment of solving a crime feels like a lightning bolt to the brain. Sudden. Dazzling. Irreversible. As a lightning bolt to the brain cleaves a skull in two, revealing the once-hidden mind within, a certain insight cracks open the mystery. What is now seen cannot be unseen.

It is a revelation.

She knew who'd taken the staff, and she knew what she ought to do about it. She also knew she didn't want to. She held still for a moment, deciding. She wasn't deciding what she had to do. Rather, she was deciding who she was—and who she wanted to be.

That was a great deal more difficult.

33

The Thief Unmasked

Amelia MacGuffin had been gathering clues all along. She hadn't realized it as it happened. But a part of her mind did, the mysterious, deep-down part that kept nudging the edges of a problem until the pieces snapped together.

Red hair that did not belong to one of the Morse twins.

The smear of mud she hadn't paid attention to when she'd originally discovered the hair.

The great interest Doc had in the hedge between the MacGuffin house and Dr. Agatha's.

The curious movement of the hedge when she'd been drinking tea with Dr. Agatha.

The number of times Doc had gotten himself exceedingly muddy while doing his business outside.

The nature of the things the thief had taken. A stick. Toys. Soft blankets. A flying disc.

She knew exactly what sort of thief those would delight. A dog. Her dog. She had to find him. And she had a very good idea where she would. And all of that knowing meant that she had decided who she was and what story she would write with her choices. It meant she had to do the thing she least wanted to do. But that was the person she wanted to be: honest and brave.

Amelia sprinted toward home. She hadn't said goodbye to anyone, although with every beat of her heart as she ran, she felt the word. *Goodbye, goodbye, goodbye.* It was like a bell, like a hammer, like a hillside splitting in two.

"Amelia! Amelia!"

People called her name, no doubt wondering why she'd shot off like a rabbit on a rocket. She had to ignore them, at least for now.

By the time she reached the MacGuffin house, she was winded. She didn't bother opening the gate. She put a hand on the fence and vaulted over it. Then she ran around back.

"Doc!"

She needed to see him, needed to know, even as she did not know what she would do with the certainty.

There was no sign of him. She studied the hedge. There—a tuft of fur. She examined each color in the clump, including a single red strand like the one she'd found earlier.

She dropped to her knees. The squishy grass soaked her jeans. Deep in the green, she spotted movement. She crawled through the branches, wincing as they scraped her. In the center of the hedge was a deep hole in the ground, and in that deep hole was Doc.

All around him were things that had been missing: the original dragonfly staff, the fake dragonfly staff, the twins' half blankets, the flying disc, and so much more. There was also a chewed and dirty piece of rope, the one he'd been tied up with.

The thief was Doc. *Doc was the thief.* She hadn't suspected him. Not for a moment, not until he and the fake dragonfly staff had disappeared at the same time. That was when it fell into place. Edith Phipps, PhD, had been exactly right about the feeling that came with it, though she'd said nothing of the heartbreak that followed.

Amelia had solved the crime. But instead of feeling happy, she was wrecked. She had solved it too late, and the solution would have consequences. There was no way her family would want to keep Doc now. He would go from being the town celebrity to the town villain. Probably no one would want to adopt him because who would want a dog that steals?

And if no one adopted him—

Amelia wouldn't let herself finish that thought. She knew exactly what happened to dogs no one wanted. She crawled into the hole with Doc and wept.

34

This Is How It Ends

She hadn't been there long before someone slid the handle of a shovel into the hole and nudged her.

"You, Amelia MacGuffin." It was Dr. Agatha.

"Yes?" Amelia tried to make it sound as though she had not been weeping.

"It can't be as bad as all that." And then Dr. Agatha's face was through the shrubs. "Ouch. Ach. This is no place for a girl and her dog and— Oh. I see. I'd suspected as much."

"It wasn't me," Amelia said.

"Of course it wasn't you. It was that dog of yours. The hedge has been wriggling ever since he moved in. I thought at first it was some sort of wild animal. A raccoon. An oversize possum."

Dr. Agatha pushed her glasses up her nose. "But then I saw him streak in there with something in his mouth a few days back. To be honest, I didn't think much of it. What is it to me if a dog has a toy? I'm not opposed to any creature's enjoyment. Although that did remind me of the time I'd seen him around Glenda. You asked if I saw a person near the Sasquatch statue. I did not. But I did see a dog. *That* dog."

"The red hair was his," Amelia said. "Not one of the Morse twins'."

"Ha-ha. A red hairing that was not a red herring," Dr. Agatha said.

Amelia didn't laugh. None of this was funny.

"Well, you must feel terrific at having apprehended the thief," Dr. Agatha said. "You're not half bad as a detective."

"I wish I hadn't cracked the case," she said.

"You'll find another one soon enough," Dr. Agatha said. "Mark my words."

Amelia put her face in her hands and sobbed. Dr. Agatha didn't understand. Amelia didn't miss having a mystery to solve. She grieved the solution to this one and always would.

"There, there," Dr. Agatha said.

Amelia had never understood why that was supposed to console someone. Why not *here, here* or *where, where*?

"Things always look better on the outside of a hedge," Dr. Agatha said. "Come on out. Your criminal mastermind canine too. We'll get you cleaned up and back to the festival."

"There isn't going to be a festival," Amelia said. "There was a mudslide."

"Oh," Dr. Agatha said. "That explains the ruckus. I thought somebody had dropped a bowling ball down the new town stairs."

"When my parents find out Doc is the thief, they won't let us keep him," Amelia said. "And no one in town will want a dog that steals. And it's Doc's fault the town lost its luck, and the mudslide wrecked the festival. He's also made us all suspicious and unpleasant. There will be no coming back from this. Doc'll be cast aside as a villain. He will never have a family. He's a goner." Her heart was broken. She could not imagine it ever being fixed.

Dr. Agatha sighed. Then she crawled all the way into the hole with Amelia, grunting and creaking as she went. "These are all terrible things," she said when she settled herself in. "But maybe it won't be as bad as all that."

Doc put his head in Dr. Agatha's lap and looked up at her with his unusually large brown eyes. "You do look like trouble," she said sternly. "But I've always had a soft spot for a scoundrel."

Amelia snuffled. "In your books, what happens to the bad guys when they get caught?"

"Typically that's when books end," Dr. Agatha said. "That's the whole point of a mystery. To solve the crime. To catch the guilty party. Other people write books about lawyers and the court, but that's not my cup of tea."

Amelia wasn't sure what kind of person would want to read about lawyers and courts. It sounded terribly dull.

"Does anybody ever get away with a crime?" Amelia asked.

"In real life, all the time," Dr. Agatha said. "And some things that should be crimes aren't, and some things that shouldn't be crimes are."

"That doesn't seem fair," Amelia said.

Dr. Agatha put her arm around Amelia. "And it isn't. I suppose that's why I write mysteries. I can always decide how they end. I get to make things fair in stories that might not be in real life."

"Is this story over?" Amelia asked. "Is Doc going to the pound? Is he going to . . ." She could not say the word.

"I don't know," Dr. Agatha said. "But not if I can help it. Have you ever read my book *Let Sleeping Bulldozers Lie*?"

Amelia felt embarrassed. She hadn't read any of Dr. Agatha's books, though she'd heard plenty about them. Her parents said that murder and sherry were for grown-ups.

"It's not important," Dr. Agatha said. "But you should know that I always do a great deal of research when I write."

"I've seen you browsing the nonfiction section at the library," Amelia said.

"You don't miss much, do you?" She tapped Amelia's nose. "Come on. Grab the staff. We'll clean up at my house. I'll make a quick call, and then we'll do what needs to be done."

Amelia didn't want to. But at least she didn't have to do it alone. She had Doc, and she had Dr. Agatha, who most definitely was *not* a murderer. She was turning out to be a most unlikely friend.

With the staff in one hand and Doc's leash in the other, Amelia crawled out of the hedge and emerged on Dr. Agatha's lawn.

35

Amelia Does the Right Thing

Dr. Agatha made Amelia and Doc wait on the porch.

"It's for his own safety," she said. "Crumpet doesn't care for dogs. In his eyes, they're all criminals."

A couple of minutes later, she opened the door and handed Amelia a bucket of warm water, some soap, a washcloth, and a clean cardigan that smelled like the stuff Mrs. MacGuffin sometimes used on the twins' bottoms. Then Dr. Agatha reached into the pocket of her own cardigan and handed Amelia a comb.

"Here," she said. "Your hair—it could use some help."

Amelia dunked Doc's paws into the bucket, which was the same kind they carried at the Pacific General Store. The store. Would her parents have to close it? Would they have to sell their wonderful old house? Would they have to move someplace else? Someplace without a view of the ocean and paths made of crushed oyster shells?

She wiped Doc until he was as clean as he was going to get. Then she cleaned herself and donned the cardigan. It had a fresh pack of tissues in one pocket and a tin of ginger candies in the other. Amelia loved ginger candies. She also liked small things, and a pack of tissues made for a single person counted as exactly that. Plus, she really needed to wipe her nose.

And then she considered her hair. She didn't have a mirror, but sunlight bounced off the windows and returned a wobbly version of her own reflection to her. Amelia ran the comb through her hair, parting it in the usual spot. She studied the version of herself held in the window. That was the old Amelia looking at her. The old Amelia had been changed by recent events. She'd been brave when she needed to be. She could be brave enough to do this. And so, Amelia changed the part in her hair, something she'd wanted to do for so long. She'd lost so much that mattered to her, but this was something she could have.

She finished as Dr. Agatha re-emerged from the house in a fresh cardigan that matched Amelia's. Dr. Agatha popped a ginger candy into her mouth, shifted it to her cheek, and said, "I like your hair that way. You look like a regular detective. Or at least someone who knows enough about detecting to write irresistible cozy mysteries."

Amelia decided to take it as a compliment, even as she regretted becoming a detective in the first place. Solving her first crime was going to cost Amelia her first dog.

"Well, then," Dr. Agatha said. "We could hold hands as we walk to the edge of town."

"That's okay," Amelia said. "I need one hand for the staff and one hand for Doc's leash."

"Thank goodness," Dr. Agatha said. "I am not a hand holder at all, but I thought it might make you feel better."

Amelia almost smiled. She hadn't thought it possible to feel nearly normal again. Who could, after finding out their dog is a criminal mastermind? But maybe that was the most mysterious thing about hearts: how they could break and go on beating.

"It shouldn't be long now," Dr. Agatha said.

There was something very like Bridget about Dr. Agatha. Amelia didn't love it, but she was used to bossy people who said obvious things out loud. She wished Dr. Agatha didn't sound so pleased about their pending doom.

The square was full of people, some moving their booths, some making gestures of consolation. No one noticed Amelia, Doc, and Dr. Agatha. No one noticed that Amelia held the town staff. The closer she got to everyone, though, the heavier it felt.

Amelia waved at her mother, who brought her hands to her heart as if she'd been terribly worried. Then her father, who pointed at the staff and gave her a double thumbs-up.

While she'd been gone, her family had moved the popcorn stand, helium tank, and cotton candy machine to the town square. Amelia would have bet it was Bridget's idea. Bridget knew a crowd meant money. Urchin Beach residents had already lined up for popcorn and balloons. Bridget was at her machine, muddy as ever, handing out balloons and taking cash. Amelia wondered if she was going to have to make cotton candy. She wasn't in the mood. But she would. It was a responsibility. To make good on that was what a person did for love.

"You're back!" Colin said. "Mom and Dad were worried. I wasn't. Birdie was getting ready to write an article about your disappearance until Delphine told her it was too soon."

The twins sat in a red wagon like the one her parents sold in the Pacific General Store. Each of them held a balloon. It was not enough to make them levitate, but it was enough to keep them occupied.

Amelia looked at the staff. Now that it was back, at least some things were starting to feel right again. But the hardest part was yet to come.

"I'll be back in a bit," Amelia said.

Amelia, Doc, and Dr. Agatha kept walking until they reached

Mayor Hoffman, who stood a few feet away from Officer Shirley Locke. They were talking with each other on walkie-talkies.

"Excuse me, Mayor Hoffman," Amelia said. "But I have something." She handed over the staff.

The mayor's eyes widened. "Where did you find this? Oh, I'm so relieved. The one your dad found on the beach might have fooled some people, but it didn't fool me. I was playing along with it to be a good sport because an effective leader needs to be one more often than you'd expect. But I am so happy to have the real dragonfly staff back."

"I knew you'd get it back, my sweet bowl of breakfast cereal," Mr. Jung said. He blew the mayor a kiss.

Amelia looked at Dr. Agatha, who nodded in encouragement. "Tell her what you discovered," Dr. Agatha said.

"It was hidden," Amelia said.

She looked at Doc and felt as though she was betraying him. This was so awful. But what choice did she have? He'd done it. He'd committed a crime. She thought about what her dad had said about crimes.

Mr. MacGuffin wasn't an expert, like Dr. Agatha's sister, who'd written a whole book about them. But what he'd said made sense to her now.

Sometimes people take things without knowing they're important. Sometimes people take things because they need them. Sometimes it's because they're hurting or even angry. All of that was true about Doc. Well, maybe not the part about him being angry. He was wagging his tail, even now.

But this moment wasn't only about who Doc was and what he'd lived through. This moment was about Amelia MacGuffin, and she knew who she wanted to be. Someone brave enough to tell the truth, even when it was hard. Even when it cost her something she loved.

"My dog hid it," she said. "Well, not *my* dog, but the dog our family is taking care of for the time being. I don't think he knew it was special. But it wasn't all he took. All of the missing stuff in town is in his lair."

"His lair?" Officer Locke pulled out her notebook and a pen.

"He dug a hole in a hedge and hid stuff there. He's a thief and that's where he hides out, so I think *lair* is the proper word for it."

"I agree," Dr. Agatha said. "It's a lair."

Birdie approached, her own notebook and pencil in hand.

Colin and Bridget rushed up too. Their parents and the twins were close behind. "Dot and Dash are childing the popcorn and balloon stations," Colin said.

"Manning," Bridget said. "They're middle schoolers, not children."

"Did someone say 'lair'?" Mr. MacGuffin asked.

"Lair," Duncan said.

"Lair," Emma said.

Amelia felt her lower lip give way. Dr. Agatha gave Amelia's hand a quick squeeze using a finger and thumb. This was not comforting, but Amelia appreciated the effort.

"Mom and Dad," Amelia said, "it was Doc. He stole the staff. And Duncan's and Emma's half blankets. And a whole lot of other stuff."

Duncan and Emma burst into tears at the mention of their blankets. Amelia started crying too. She should have thought to bring those along. She couldn't get anything right.

"Doc did it?" Mr. MacGuffin said.

"I never would have suspected him," Mrs. MacGuffin said.

"That's because you're a seller of dry goods and not a writer of mysteries," Dr. Agatha said.

"How did you figure it out, Amelia?" Colin asked.

"She's a detective, duh," Bridget said.

"That's the headline," Birdie said. "'Urchin Beach's Kid Detective Solves Crime Spree.'"

Amelia was crying so hard she almost couldn't speak. But she had to because she had to know how the story was going to end. "Does this mean we have to send Doc to the pound?"

"No, please, no!" Colin said.

"You wouldn't!" Bridget said.

"This is something we can talk about later," Mr. MacGuffin said.

"Let's not spoil the fun," Mrs. MacGuffin said.

What fun? Amelia wanted to say. This was not fun, and a person didn't need to be a detective to know that.

Before anyone could say anything else, though, there was a rumble. But it was not the rumble of sliding mud. No, it was the rumble of something mechanical, deep and throaty.

Dr. Agatha lifted her index finger in the air, as if she were testing the breeze or about to make an important point. Then she turned toward the WELCOME TO URCHIN BEACH sign.

County police cars approached, their lights flashing. For a moment, Amelia thought they'd come to arrest Doc. Then she noticed the bulldozer behind them, its mud-spattered bucket raised high. Behind it was the longest line of cars Amelia had ever seen—cars full of tourists who'd finally made their way to the festival.

"Well," Dr. Agatha said. "That's better than a sharp poke in the eye."

The mayor turned to Amelia. "Take the staff for a minute. Keep it safe."

Amelia held on tight.

36

Just Deserts (Plus Balloons, Popcorn, and Cotton Candy)

"And this is why we always do our research," Dr. Agatha said.

Dr. Agatha explained that when she'd written *Let Sleeping Bulldozers Lie*, she'd needed to learn all sorts of information about bulldozers. The villain of the book had hidden a body in the upraised bucket of one.

In doing this research, Dr. Agatha said, she had not only learned that bulldozers could clear away a great deal of mud. She'd also acquainted herself with a bulldozer operator who lived on the other side of the slide. The county police cruisers that Amelia worried had come for Doc had been guiding cars to the side of the road so that the bulldozer could get through. Now that the road was clear of mud, car after car full of tourists could make it to Urchin Beach. There was going to be a Dragonfly Day Festival after all.

"These new arrivals are going to want balloons," Bridget announced.

"And popcorn," Colin said. "The smell alone is sure to draw ravenous hordes."

"I'm going to make a killing," Bridget said.

But she did not mean the kind of killing that would interest a detective or the writer of mysteries. She meant a whole lot of money. Even Colin understood.

"And I bet I see the first dragonfly too," Bridget said.

Bridget was wrong about that, Amelia knew. But she was probably right about the money. It would be enough to cover the costs of the equipment and then some—but probably not enough to keep Doc. That would take more balloons than Bridget had.

Amelia watched crowds of people emerge from cars. She decided to ask one of the Morse twins, or possibly both, to youth the machine for a few minutes. They were no doubt up to the task.

For now, Amelia couldn't bear to leave Doc. Not when there were police and Officer Shirley Locke and Mayor Hoffman and, worse, her parents, milling about and deciding Doc's fate. Whatever happened to this dog, she would be there to witness it. And if Birdie was going to write an article about what a bad dog he was, Amelia would insist on being quoted this time, telling readers about what he'd suffered in the past and how good he'd been. Well, except for the stealing.

Amelia crouched by his side, still holding the dragonfly staff. Doc licked her cheek and the inside of her ear, which felt so weird she would have giggled if his fate weren't hanging in the balance.

Mayor Hoffman sat on the ground next to her. "I'm probably going to regret this," the mayor said. "Getting up isn't as easy as it used to be. Knees should come with a warranty."

Amelia said, "If you get stuck, I can help pull you back on your feet."

"You did an excellent job solving the Case of the Missing Dragonfly Staff," Mayor Hoffman said. "And it had to be hard to learn that your dog—well, the dog your family is taking care of—is the guilty party."

Amelia nodded. It was hard. She understood what the mayor meant by *guilty party*, even as it sounded like something she never wanted to be invited to again.

"This is what I think about the case," the mayor said. "I think we have our staff back. I also think that we never really lost it. It was in Urchin Beach all along, and even though it seemed like the storms and the collapse of the staircase and then the mudslide were proof that Urchin Beach's luck had been stolen, that's not what the evidence says."

"It's not?" Amelia asked.

"It's not," Mayor Hoffman said. "Because what do you see right in front of your eyes?"

She saw people. Her family. The Morses. Maya. Birdie and Delphine. Kat, Hayden, and Eugenides. Townspeople and tourists eating popcorn and holding balloons and taking the stairs down to the beach to play games and listen to music before the parade started. The knot inside her, the one that made talking impossible without sobbing, was starting to come loose. Was this how it felt when Doc shed the rope around his neck? Like the relief of dawn pushing away the darkness of night?

The mayor nodded. "That's right. The luck was here all along. The things we couldn't control—like the weather and the pull of gravity—those are part of life. But when we needed people—people to rebuild stairs and patch roofs and call bulldozers and move mud—well, we had everyone we needed when we needed them. Crabby or not, we had everyone we needed."

"That's true," Dr. Agatha said. "And if I hadn't found Amelia and Doc in the hedge lair, I wouldn't have known to call the bulldozer operator."

"And we wouldn't have been in the hedge lair," Amelia said, "if Doc hadn't taken the staff from the mayor."

"That's a whole lot of luck, all strung together," Mayor Hoffman said. "Not to mention all the smarts you showed in following Doc, and the courage you showed in telling us the truth. Those things are even more important than luck."

The knot inside her chest came all the way loose, and Amelia took the deepest breath she'd had in days. She looked at her parents. "Please don't give away Doc because of this. Please, let's find him a good, safe home where he's loved."

"I'll take him," Officer Shirley Locke said. "I've always liked dogs. And I could teach him not to steal."

"The library could use a dog," Miss Fortune said. "There's nothing quite like reading with a dog snoring at your feet."

Bonnie from the knitting shop spoke up next. "Did you know some people make yarn out of dog hair? He'd be such an asset for the shop. I'll take him."

"Aw, Bonnie," said Clyde, the grocer. "If you let me have him, I'll save everything he sheds for you. Or we could, I don't know, share him." He wheeled himself closer to her.

"I have no interest in the dog," Dr. Agatha said. "I am very much committed to Crumpet."

"Wow," Mayor Hoffman said. "It seems as though almost everyone in Urchin Beach wants Doc for their very own."

"But I'm afraid that's impossible," Mr. MacGuffin said.

Amelia held her breath. Surely her parents couldn't want to take Doc to the pound.

"Doc already has a home," Mrs. MacGuffin said. "He has a home with us."

"But what about the cost?" Amelia asked. "How will we afford him?"

"I'll chip in," Clyde said.

"Me too," Bonnie said.

"Nonsense," Mr. Jung said. "He's going to be the mascot of Urchin Beach's Forever Jung Realty. Everybody likes dogs. I'll pay for his up-keep—provided I don't have to touch him or live with him. I'm allergic."

Mayor Hoffman planted a kiss on Mr. Jung's lips. "I love you, you horrible goat."

Amelia felt as though her sister had inflated an irresponsible number of helium balloons and attached them to her heart. A huge swell of hope and happiness rose through her body, and if she hadn't been sitting on the ground holding on to Doc, she would not have been surprised if she soared straight into the brilliant blue sky.

The MacGuffin family had a dog. They had Doc. That one final spot in their family, the one empty piece of the puzzle, was finally in place. And everyone in town was looking out for him.

"How about this," the mayor said. "I issue a proclamation: Doc is the official mascot of all of Urchin Beach, not just the Realty. And what that means is, for as long as he's here, wherever he is, he's home."

Doc barked. Amelia could swear it was because he understood.

Mayor Hoffman wasn't finished. "Doc is our official mascot. You are our official youth detective. Urchin Beach is extremely fortunate to have you both. And now let's get this parade started. This year, and for the first time ever, I believe we will have a dog as our grand marshal. Now, who's going to help me stand?"

Amelia offered the mayor a hand. When Doc heard the word *stand*, he rose on his hind legs, just as she'd imagined. And as he stood there, like a highly accomplished dog, something featherlight landed on top of his head. A green darner dragonfly. The first of the day.

Amelia lifted it on her finger. "Look!" she said. "Look! The first green darner. It found Doc!"

She started to cry again. But this time, it was tears of joy.

Bridget put her arm around her. "I knew we'd see one," she said. "They just needed a little help. While you were solving the crime, I thought I'd make myself useful. I've been restoring their habitat. I even did some of it while standing on my hands. And Eugenides helped. Did you know he isn't half bad?"

"Oh, Bridget," Amelia said.

She loved her sister. She would always make sure there was enough room on the path for both of them. And for all the MacGuffins. For everybody.

37

The Thief at Home
(At Last)

The thief was confused at first, when the terrible noise started. Oh, how it hurt his ears. There was a whining sound. And then the crunching of sticks. Was a monster eating his cozy den?

He barked and looked out the window into the backyard. The hedge quivered. Something was coming through it, something noisy and terrifying. He watched, his ears pointed as if on high alert.

The MacGuffin children noticed and arranged themselves around him.

"It's all right, Doc. It's Dr. Agatha."

And sure enough, it was. She emerged through the hedge wearing safety goggles and holding the terrible machine, which he learned was called a chain saw. She cut a hole in the hedge where his hideaway had been. She made an opening. A space for people and dogs to walk through. A connection between two homes that had been divided.

An open doorway made through living hedge was even better than a lair. And while he did miss his treasures, he was glad to have them returned to their owners.

"Why'd you do it, boy?" Amelia had asked.

He didn't have the words to tell her. But the moment he'd arrived in Urchin Beach, he'd seen the staff. He knew it would change his life if he took it. He leaned against her. She smelled like books. Like cocoa. Like bubble baths. Like love. Which was enough, all by itself, and always had been. It's what every one of his treasures had smelled like, and who was he—who was anyone—to resist that?

Even as he'd felt ashamed when he'd been caught, he couldn't regret taking the staff. He couldn't regret taking anything.

He couldn't regret what he'd done because it had brought him to the MacGuffin family, the thing he'd wished for all those days and nights tied up to a tree, forgotten and uncared for. He'd been hungry and thirsty, not just for food and water, but for this life. This life in the heart of a very large family. This life, where he was loved.

And truly, he hadn't *stolen* the staff. He'd only borrowed it for a little while.

Now that he had what he needed, he'd never steal again. He looked at Amelia. At Bridget and Colin. At the little twins. He might have stolen a few things here and there, but they had stolen his heart.

It seemed like a fair trade.

Urchin Beach Detective
Agency Opens

by Birdie Wheeler, ~~Staff Writer~~ News Intern

DRAFT

The MacGuffin Detective Agency is open for business in Urchin Beach. Founder Amelia MacGuffin, age eleven, is best known locally for solving the Case of the Missing Dragonfly Staff. (It turned out her dog took it.)

MacGuffin will charge $5 per day plus expenses for her work.

"No crime is too small," she said. "But some might be too scary."

"Don't be ridiculous," sister Bridget MacGuffin said. "You're the bravest person I know."

"Murder is terrifying," brother Colin MacGuffin said.

"Murder," siblings Duncan and Emma MacGuffin said.

"No one is getting murdered in Urchin Beach," Officer Shirley Locke said.

Cut.

Birdie, this detracts from your story.

Don't crush my thunder, Mom. That's color. It's pure gold.

I'm not your mom. I'm your editor.

Okay.

"But in case they do," Colin MacGuffin said, "Amelia will solve it."

"Unless she's the one who got murdered," Bridget said.

"Bridget," all the MacGuffins said.

"What, it's true," Bridget said.

Amelia MacGuffin said she founded the agency to solve complicated cases that Officer Locke doesn't have time to handle.

"So far, theft is my specialty," Amelia MacGuffin said. "But I am open to all sorts of mysteries. Missing people and pets. Buried treasures. Even hauntings."

To hire MacGuffin and her assistant, a mixed-breed dog named Doc, leave a note for her at the Pacific General Store. She will be in touch within twenty-four hours.

(Reporter's note: Amelia MacGuffin is one of my best friends, but this article isn't biased. It's 100 percent true. Amelia is the best detective in town. You can ask anyone.)

Acknowledgments

It should be no mystery that books are created by teams and not authors working alone. It would be a crime for me to fail to acknowledge the hard work that went into making this beautiful book.

To my agent, Jennifer Laughran, for supporting whatever I hurl into your inbox, thank you.

Thank you to my editor, Jody Corbett. You have earned a key to Urchin Beach.

To Melissa Schirmer, our production editor; Stephanie Yang, our designer; and Monika Wiśniewska, our cover artist: I am so grateful for your skills and hard work.

And to the rest of the team at Scholastic for supporting my work for more than a decade: David Levithan, Ellie Berger, Erin Berger, Seale Ballenger, Lia Ferrone, Lizette Serrano, Emily Heddleson, Sabrina Montenigro, Maisha Johnson, Meredith Wardell, Rachel

Feld, Katie Dutton, Kelsey Albertson, Holly Alexander, Julie Beckman, Tracy Bozentka, Savannah D'Amico, Sarah Herbik, Roz Hilden, Barbara Holloway, Brigid Martin, Liz Morici, Dan Moser, Nikki Mutch, Sydney Niegos, Caroline Noll, Debby Owusu-Appiah, Bob Pape, Jacqueline Perumal, Betsy Politi, Jackie Rubin, Chris Satterlund, Terribeth Smith, Jody Stigliano, Sarah Sullivan, Melanie Wann, Jarad Waxman, and Elizabeth Whiting.

I'm lucky to have a group of friends always willing to read drafts, scratch my head, and tell me I'm good: Elana K. Arnold, Liz Garton Scanlon, Jolie Stekly, Michele Bacon, Ann Haywood Leal, and all the rest of the Frosting Heads.

To Kate Messner, Linda Urban, Mike Jung, Eliot Schrefer, Anne Ursu, and Justina Chen for setting the best example for all of us.

To my colleagues and students at Vermont College of Fine Arts, thank you for everything that you teach me.

To all the mystery writers I read instead of doing schoolwork, thank you. Especially you, Agatha Christie. I had a hunch you'd be more useful to me than calculus.

And to my family: all the Brockenbroughs, the Berliants, the Wildes, the McClures, and most especially to Adam, Lucy, Alice, Dottie, Millie, Addie, and Beezus. Your love is everything and I don't even mind it when you barf on me.

About the Author

Martha Brockenbrough is the critically acclaimed author of numerous chapter books, picture books, young adult novels, and nonfiction titles. *To Catch a Thief* is her first novel for middle-grade readers. She teaches at Vermont College of Fine Arts and lives in Seattle, Washington, with her husband, their two daughters, two dogs, and two cats. You can visit her online at marthabrockenbrough.com.